GUIDEPOSTS

CHURCH CHOIR
MYSTERIES™

Puzzle in
Patchwork

Roberta Updegraff

Guideposts®

CARMEL, NEW YORK 10512

www.guidepostsbooks.com

www.guidepostsbooks.com
Series Editor: Michele Slung
Cover art by Robert Tanenbaum
Cover design by Wendy Bass
Interior design by José R. Fonfrias
Interior cat illustrations by Viqui Maggio
Typeset by Composition Technologies, Inc.
Printed in the United States of America

To my mothers:

Evelyn Taylor Updegraff, mother of my heart. She, too, has stitched fabric and soul, creating heirloom quilts we will all treasure forever.

And my mother, Betty O'Dwyer Blair.

Acknowledgments

DURING THE COURSE of writing this book, I lost a dear friend. Hazel Shade Sinclair embodied Sophie and gave Abe Wasserman his Jewish wit. She and her husband Harold have celebrated Christmas with us, and we Passover with them. We've shared our lives and our faith, much the same way as Gracie and Abe do in this series. We will miss Hazel very much.

I am also thankful to the Updegraff family for their long-ago participation in the Underground Railroad. There is an escape tunnel in our family homestead here in Williamsport, Pennsylvania.

Thanks to Sandy Campbell, my Indiana resource person, and to Robin Leidhecker for providing genealogical and courthouse protocol. And as always, I appreciate my friends in the West Branch Christian Writers group and St. David's Christian Writers' Conference.

Kudos to my great editors at Guideposts Book and Inspirational Media Division! Thanks, Elizabeth Kramer Gold and Michele Slung and Stephanie Castillo Samoy, for all your support.

Puzzle in Patchwork

"IT WILL BE THRILLING!" Cordelia Fountain beamed, exhibiting an excitement that in one of Willow Bend's grandest dames was not to be taken lightly. The tourist home owner wore her blue bouffant like a crown, and majestically chose to observe many old-fashioned niceties of etiquette.

Gracie Parks delighted in the older woman's fervor, and recognized that Cordelia was in her element as head of the planning committee for Willow Bend's upcoming Founders' Day Celebration. Their beloved community would soon be celebrating its bicentennial birthday, and Eternal Hope Community Church now was hosting the opening reception.

"Eternal Hope's Family Center is truly a blessing, with all this space and its modern kitchen, too." Cordelia made a graceful sweep of her arm. "It kicks off our celebration with an acknowledgment of our Christian heritage. That, to me, is important."

It did seem fitting to be launching Willow Bend's journey into its second century in one of the local churches. After all, their ancestors had recognized the importance of religion by constructing their places of worship as soon as they settled an area, with towns growing up around them. For her part, Gracie was always glad to see her church and her community working together. That harmony had been one of her late husband's goals when the church had decided to expand its facility. Elmo had felt the new Family Center should not only serve the church, but also the community. As a respected elder, he had made his opinions clear. Thankfully, the church board had agreed and had constructed the large addition with the idea that it would accommodate a variety of events and celebrations.

"Friendship and compassion are the best evangelistic tools," Elmo Parks would say. Yes, her adored El would have been proud to be a part of such a wonderful occasion. She herself had always been so proud of him. And when he'd been elected mayor, El had been no ordinary stuffy town dignitary. She smiled inwardly. With his collar button open and tie askew, he was the kind of guy to roll up his sleeves and wash dishes at the end of community affairs.

And there's not a day goes by I don't miss him, Lord. She closed her eyes a moment for heavenly comfort.

"Gracie?" Cordelia's face registered concern.

"I was thinking of El, of how he loved to be at the

center of things. And our church was at the heart of his life."

"Your husband was not just a good mayor," Cordelia said, placing a hand on Gracie's shoulder, "but a good friend. We all miss him, my dear."

Gracie was touched by her friend's words.

"Everyone has been so helpful!" Cordelia said, changing the subject. "And your uncle's offer to construct the panels for our genealogy display was a godsend."

Her clear blue eyes met Gracie's. "I'm sure Elmo would have done the same."

Now, that was funny! "You wouldn't have wanted El to construct panels! Uncle Miltie used to say my husband would cut a board twice and still wonder why it was too short."

"George is quite a character. With a sense of humor all his own." She pointed to the two five-foot high tri-fold panels decorated with old family photographs and biographies. "He came to see me before he constructed them. I was polite enough to laugh at most—not all, though, I assure you—of his jokes."

Gracie shook her head, thinking her uncle probably had enjoyed trying out his corniest punchlines on the determinedly staid Cordelia Fountain. George Morgan, alias Uncle Miltie to everyone in town, wasn't as unaware of his audience as one might suppose. After all, he was nicknamed for a famous—and very successful—comedian.

"Great job, Mrs. Fountain!" Pastor Paul Meyer joined

them. "I love parties, and birthdays are just my favorite!"

"Birthdays are special," Gracie agreed. "They honor life."

"And I'm all for that," Cordelia rejoined. "Aches aside, I'm grateful for every day the Lord offers me." She laughed. "It doesn't even matter that now when I stoop to tie my shoes, I wonder what else I can do while I'm down there."

Gracie chuckled at the truth in that. The body surrenders to aging, that was true, but the spirit remains indomitable. Spiritually, they would all be eternally young. As Uncle Miltie was fond of saying, "Willow Bend is the closest place to paradise this side of the Pearly Gates."

Paul offered his hand to Cordelia. "I just want to thank you again for your organizing efforts. This is a wonderful kick-off and I look forward to Founder's Day."

He gave Gracie an encouraging wink. "Now, if you'll excuse me, I'm going to mingle with the crowd—maybe find a newcomer looking for a church family."

"Such a nice man," Cordelia said, watching as he shook hands with a young couple.

Gracie agreed.

"Ah, we're probably on the same train of thought." Cordelia flashed a complicitous smile. "Who can I match up with Willow Bend's handsomest unmarried minister? I was thinking of that sweet girl who does my hair."

Gracie laughed. "Pastor Paul has dodged our best-made matches. I think he likes being single."

"Nonsense, he just hasn't met the right girl."

Those were Gracie's feelings exactly.

"Well, I see our good mayor over there. I want to talk to him when he's alone. He hasn't addressed our recommendation for those landmark plaques—the Historical District Preservation Committee has readied a list we want him to look at."

When Cordelia put her mind to something she was a force with which to be reckoned. As the owner of a large Victorian house, she had lobbied for an ordinance protecting the town's historic dwellings. To preserve the Victorian character of Main Street, she had even convinced Willow Bend to install reproduction gas street lights. The city council practically never knew what hit them.

"This is a great turnout," commented Marybeth Bower, as she appeared beside them at the refreshment table. This Eternal Hope choir soprano was married to the town's chief of police. She'd traded in her second-grade classroom for the opportunity to home-school her twins.

The twins seemed a mismatched duo, opposites in about every respect. Corey was all boy, and Casey feminine to a T. The only similarity they seemed to share was the sprinkling of freckles across the bridges of their noses.

Gracie recalled that Marybeth was quite interested in genealogy. "I haven't studied Willow Bend's latest family album—what should I especially look for?"

"Keep an eye out for Ames, Simmonses, Carsons and Taylors—we go way back." She fixed herself a cup of lemonade punch and offered one to Cordelia. "I've been meaning to talk to you about that. You know I found some 'new' pieces recently—heirlooms—a journal and a quilt belonging to my great-great grandmother."

Cordelia nodded, as she received her cup, but before she could comment, Don Delano joined them.

"Gracie is simply the best caterer in the county!" Don exclaimed, reaching for one of the cups. He toasted Gracie. "Make that the state!"

Gracie felt herself blush.

"Everyone's here—practically half the town!" Don said, glancing around. "I'm sure almost the whole church has turned out!"

"Willow Bend is the envy of the county," Cordelia couldn't help but boast. "It's not only the center of the county, but the prettiest place in Indiana."

Gracie raised her cup in agreement. "Hear! Hear!"

"I hate what they're doing over in Avery." Marybeth told them. "They're putting in another one of those mini-malls. I mean really, how many of those does a community need? They all have exactly the same stores!"

Cordelia agreed with this, too. "Avery was such a lovely little place." She glanced at Gracie. "You know, there is actually some minor dispute about which town is older. Willow Bend and Avery applied for their charters at the same time, but Willow Bend's was processed first, so we have that grand distinction."

Don excused himself to stop Sue Jameson, the attractive and *single* features editor at the *Mason County Gazette*. Gracie smiled, finding the lively Sue an interesting possible match for Eternal Hope's baritone bachelor chemistry teacher.

"Some people might say we're too small-town," Marybeth interjected, "but my family has been here for generations. Small is beautiful. It gives me a sense of security."

Although Gracie had lived in Willow Bend most of her life now, she never stopped learning about this corner of Indiana she loved to call home. She and El had made the town their home right after they were married. It seemed the perfect place to raise a family. And so it became, and their church was like a family to them, as well.

"Willow Bend presides over our landscape and our lives like a wise old woman," Cordelia began, as though she was giving one of those genealogical talks for which she was famous. "One who's perfectly comfortable with herself."

"Because it's the longest-established town in the county?" Marybeth, ever logical, wanted to know.

"Maturity has little to do with age, my dear." Cordelia herself was serene. "It's spiritual." She paused to take a sip of her punch.

Gracie sampled hers. This was one of her favorite recipes,

a lemonade and ginger-ale mix with just a hint of mint, decorated with sugar-frosted lemon slices and sprigs of fresh spearmint. So refreshing!

"Our little town has taken some tough stands over the years, most recently when it came to protecting our community from industrial exploitation," Cordelia continued. "That's a manifestation of our spirit, of which, it goes without saying, I am very proud."

Gracie followed Cordelia's gaze around the room. Folks milled about and chatted amiably. They were her chosen family. They had been there to support her when her husband was killed in a car accident. She recalled special moments of encouragement. *I am blessed, Lord. It seems Your most precious gifts are wrapped in flesh.*

Marybeth changed the subject. "Well, like everyone else here, I'm looking forward to all the events you have scheduled leading up to our actual birthday. Cordelia, Willow Bend is blessed to have you. And we know it."

The three women turned to the tables, where a collection of memorabilia was displayed. Although the exhibit would eventually be housed at the library, Cordelia had decided a sneak preview might encourage other residents to lend items of similar interest.

Gracie now noticed one of Willow Bend's most solitary residents slip in the entrance leading from the church proper. Charlie Harris wasn't as smart as some people, but he was a true entrepreneur. He collected and recycled aluminum cans and bottles, and could be found helping out at local businesses. He did odd jobs, as well, and seemed to like yard work all year long, weather permitting.

Some folks said it was Charlie's green thumb that made the Fountain geraniums so spectacular, even though Cordelia claimed, rather, that she owed the garden's success to her own special compost mix.

"Yoo-hoo, Charlie!" Cordelia called.

He seemed a bit uncomfortable having attention drawn to himself, but made his way to where they were standing by the display tables. He toyed with his battered felt hat while Cordelia informed him that she had taken it upon herself to fix his denim jacket. She reminded him of his cholesterol, and told him to go easy on the chocolate cake. Gracie couldn't help thinking the woman acted more like his relative than his employer. Or his landlady, which she also was.

"I'm so glad you came!" She told him. "Remember?" She extended her hand. "I'm Gracie Parks." He stuck out a thin brown arm, giving her a shy grin.

His handshake was timid at first, then stronger. She recalled how her husband based his first impressions on handshakes. He would have liked the warm, calloused feel of Charlie Harris's weathered palm. "A dependable man," El would have judged him. Gracie decided the same.

"What's on your schedule today?" Cordelia asked him. He

answered briefly and when he did look at Cordelia, Gracie caught the fondness in his eyes. He didn't seem offended by her nagging at all.

"Trees, Mizz Cordelia," he told her. And to Gracie, "The trees in the churchyard, ma'am. There's dead wood—storm loosened, I reckon. The pastor can count on me."

He shook his head. "Don't want nobody hurt."

Gracie recalled the dangling limbs in several of the trees outside. "Yes, I know the ones you mean. They seem to be inviting an accident."

"Inviting a lawsuit, is probably more like it," Marybeth said with disgust. "People are litigation-happy these days, even in Willow Bend. I'm glad you saw the problem, Mr. Harris."

Charlie's "thank you" was polite. He promptly excused himself, ambled over to the exhibit, but kept to the edge of the crowd.

"I've never had much chance to talk to Charlie," Gracie confessed, watching him look at the exhibit. "I knew he lives with you." She focused back on Cordelia. "I guess I never realized you were so close."

"Charlie has rented one of my rooms for a while now." Cordelia didn't offer more. She called greetings to several others, then looked over at the display. "So many generous people contributed memorabilia, but I hope more will add theirs after this sneak preview."

She drew them with her to the exhibit. "It's been a dream of mine to help launch a museum here in Willow Bend. Nothing elaborate, mind you, just a small building featuring local history. I was hoping it could have been part of our bicentennial celebration."

She sighed. "But sometimes it's impossible to accomplish everything at the same time. Of course, I've not given up."

"Do you remember my mentioning an heirloom quilt?" Marybeth asked Cordelia. "The one that's been in my family for over a century and a half?"

Cordelia's expression brightened. "Yes, dear, I do recall. It was your ancestress Velina Ames, I believe, who created that quilt." Before Marybeth could add more history, Cordelia continued, "Are you thinking of lending it to the display?

"I did want to discuss it with you," the police chief's wife responded.

Gracie, in the meantime, had focused her attention on the kitchen utensils, small hand tools, letters in spidery hand-writing, and other cherished items that were arranged in the exhibit. Especially striking were a battered Confederate can-teen and rifle, and a simple gray earthenware pitcher and bowl. Gracie ran her hand across the soft cool glaze of the pitcher, registering its lovely texture. She shivered, feeling for an instant its connection to the past and to the other long-ago people who had touched it, too.

"The Jackson family lent it," Cordelia said, coming up

behind her. "Its simplicity seems a little primitive compared to the other lovely antiques they own. But it's an old piece, obviously, and quite valuable."

"I like its plainness," Gracie said.

Cordelia paused to consider Gracie's comment for a moment. "The house tour we're planning," she went on, "is going to include the Jacksons'. Plus about eight others. Including mine, of course! Did I ever tell you that in my basement there's an entrance to a tunnel that was used by the Underground Railroad?"

"Many times," Gracie laughed.

Cordelia sighed. "Well, that's because the entry to the cave collapsed generations ago, leaving nothing but debris that's simply collected more over the years. Papa wanted to have it restored, but never got around to tackling it. And, unfortunately, I never could make it a priority, with so much else to attend to."

"That's too bad." Marybeth had been listening. "Something like that would make a wonderful field trip for school children. I know mine would love it. Corey is fascinated with the Civil War right now, which pleases me to no end, since history's my own favorite subject."

A kernel of an idea now crystallized, as Gracie remembered her young friend Chuckie Moon and his pals. She'd been pleased when they'd stopped in at some of the Youth Group evenings, but less so when they told her they were being treated like outsiders. (She'd wisely refrained from pointing out that it might have something to do with their preoccupation with body piercing and tattoos.) However, some sort of service project might be just the activity to draw the Eternal Hope teens closer, especially if Chuckie could be encouraged to take some responsibility for the activity. He always blossomed when he realized she, or another adult, was actually trusting him.

Gracie pictured in her mind Cordelia's stately Victorian with its welcoming front porch. Long a tourist home, its architecture and historical significance were a source of endless pride to its owner. "Would you be interested in opening the tunnel if I could rustle up a volunteer crew for you? I might be able to organize some teenagers. . . ."

"They'd have to be reliable!" Cordelia snorted. "I want none of those gangsters who hang out in my back alley. They dress very peculiarly, and Lord knows those hair colors just are not natural."

Gracie resisted the urge to remind her that her own blue tint and Gracie's red curls were not exactly the ones they themselves had been born with.

"Don't you defend them, Gracie Parks!" Cordelia warned. "I know you have a soft spot for those hooligans. But I'm sure they're the ones who stuffed my darling Wendell in the mailbox."

Gracie had to admit that she, too, suspected Chuckie and

his pals had been the ones who'd put the Fountain cat in the oversized antique mailbox. It had happened after Cordelia had called the police to complain for the umpteenth time about the boys hanging out behind her house. She'd been afraid their smoking would set the neighborhood ablaze— not that her fear was unfounded. Soon afterward began a rash of pranks that she and Officer Jim Thompson saw as revenge. It was never proved, but it helped give Chuckie's little gang a reputation they had not been able to shake, even though time had passed.

Gracie knew the boys to be honest at heart, if a bit mischievous like most teenagers. They were definitely rebellious by temperament, but at the same time straight shooters. They were actually kids a person could count on in a pinch. "I'll put out some feelers," she told Cordelia. "Perhaps we can get our Youth Group to volunteer."

Cordelia decided she wouldn't stop Gracie from pursuing the matter. In fact, it would be fascinating to see what would be unearthed. But, still, she didn't stop her grumbling about teenagers until Marybeth changed the subject back to her family quilt.

As they began to discuss the loan of it and Cordelia's idea how best to display it, Gracie let her attention drift to the task at hand—clean-up. She glanced at her watch. The event would officially be over in another ten minutes, so she began assessing the tasks at hand and mentally assigning priorities.

Marge appeared at her side. "Your trusty assistant, reporting for duty!"

Gracie handed her the stack of empty trays. Marge Lawrence was not only her next-door neighbor and catering right-hand, but also her best friend. When Gracie felt the loss of El most grievously, lamenting all they had planned but would never now share, Marge would point out to her how every end was also a beginning. "Think of all you'll have to tell El when you get to heaven," she'd remind her.

"I sure do appreciate you," Gracie said affectionately. "I hope you realize it."

"Wait until next week when the new inventory comes in." Marge winked. "I'll let you show me by helping me check it all in."

They busied themselves while departing friends stopped to compliment Gracie on the food. Cordelia bustled about, continuing to encourage people to bring things to the library, where the historical exhibit would officially reside.

Pastor Paul appeared at the kitchen door. "The folks from the historical society will pack up the display in the morning. Need anything more here?" They thanked him but assured him they could handle it.

It would take at least three trips to load Fannie Mae, Gracie's old blue Cadillac, so Marge suggested they block the door open with her weekly appointment planner. "That's probably the best use I've made of the thing." She laughed. "I always have the best intentions come the first of the year, but the entries keep getting sparser as the weeks roll in. I almost need to make an appointment to do it!"

Marge slipped the book in her pocket and double-checked the door.

"Locked?"

"Tight as a clam!"

GRACIE WAS JUST STARTING to unpack a load of groceries in her kitchen the next day when she heard the phone ring. Her inclination was to let the answering machine pick it up, but something prompted her to listen just in time to hear her pastor's frantic, "Gracie, call me—"

"Hello!"

A loud relieved sigh escaped from Eternal Hope's young and usually enthusiastic pastor. "Thank goodness you're home! Something terrible has happened!"

Gracie did a quick flip through her mental files recalling recent prayer requests. Who was sick? Having an operation? Had there been an accident? A death? Oh Lord! Sending a prayer heavenward, she asked the dreaded question: "What is it, Paul?"

"There has been a theft." The words came through the receiver with a thud.

Gracie switched the phone to the other ear and sat down on her sofa. Her cat, Gooseberry, lay at her feet, his yellow eyes wide, as though he was sensing the seriousness of the call. She coaxed him to her lap with a silent motion.

"That antique pitcher and bowl are gone."

"Are you sure someone actually stole it? Perhaps it was borrowed." Gracie preferred to remain optimistic. "Or taken home?"

"No it's been stolen, we're sure of it. Cordelia arrived with Deborah Jackson this morning to pack up the exhibit. Wouldn't you know it would be the owner of the stolen set who would be the one to come along! She wanted to make sure it was transported safely. Anyway, I was in the office and came out and offered to help, and that's when we discovered the pieces missing."

Another sigh. "I'm responsible, Gracie."

"There's got to be a reasonable explanation," she thought out loud.

Gracie had determined that human nature was a lot like everything else in life—mostly good. People could live their lives worrying about the bad apples or choose to make a pie. Gracie Parks made a lot of pies.

"I'd like to think you're right, but we've got trouble. Deborah called her husband, and he's pretty upset. He says that these things weren't really adequately covered by their homeowner's insurance. He'd had to take an extra policy."

The Jacksons were relative newcomers to Willow Bend. She knew Deborah, a nurse, had inherited the house they lived in from an aunt, and that Carl Jackson was a salesman of some sort.

"I've been praying all morning that someone would walk in with the missing things, and explain that there simply had been some miscommunication."

Gracie echoed this thought silently.

"Herb and I checked the doors a little while ago," Paul went on. "Everything was locked. I was the last one out yesterday and first one in this morning. I don't know how someone got in."

Then it hit Gracie. "You weren't the last one out. Marge and I were. We did double-check the door when we left, though."

"I was in charge." Paul was adamant. "I should have insisted we take those things to the library yesterday, or at least have had them locked up in the office. I just didn't think—"

Gracie countered, "Who would have thought they wouldn't be safe? I know it's hard, but try not to worry. She closed her eyes to settle her mind. In that brief quietness, she was reminded that the church building and the people worshiping there belonged to the Lord. "God is in control, Paul.

He will look out for His church and we must trust in that knowledge."

"I knew calling you was the right thing to do. You continue to be God's gift to me for that very reason."

Gracie loved this young minister, and couldn't resist the urge to mother him. "It's easy to get wound up in worry. I can fret my insides tight as a top. I've gotten better at trusting God over the years, thanks to my patient husband. His composure finally convinced me that things would work out—and they always did."

She could feel herself relaxing in the memory, picturing El with his arms around her. They would take strength from one another and from their belief in God's love. But a sense of humor helped, too.

Lord, thank You for Your gift of perspective.

"I'll call Herb," she told Paul. Willow Bend's strong and capable police chief could be intimidating, but whenever anything seemed to involve a crime Gracie's first instinct was always to make sure he had all the information.

"By the way, Rocky happened by. I told him I wanted to phone you and he agreed that I should. He may not think you're a gift from God the way I do, but he says you're the person he always wants by him when there's a puzzle."

Gracie grinned. Her friend the newspaper editor liked to tease her about her sleuthing habits.

"Hello, Gracie!" Herb's gruff voice came in loud and clear in spite of the static from the cell phone connection.

She grabbed a handy pad. "I just talked to Pastor Paul—"

"Gracie, do you have any ideas?" He wasn't wasting time.

"Not much, but I thought if we put our heads together we might come up with something." Gracie still felt uncertain there could have been an actual theft, nor could she guess why anyone would want the plain earthenware pitcher and bowl. Lovely as they were as objects, and valuable, too, they still seemed an unlikely target for burglars.

"When we built the addition, we had the Family Center keyed separately, so we could lock it independently and confine groups for social events," Herb reminded her. "That was my idea. The key is kept in the office, so that controls the number of people with access to it.

"Marge and I were the last ones out," she told him.

"So there's really only about an hour to account for," he calculated. "And you don't remember seeing anyone suspicious?"

Suddenly, Gracie recalled, "Marge propped the door open so we could easily make the couple of trips from the kitchen to my car. You don't suppose . . ."

She searched her memory trying to recall a car, a person, anything out of the ordinary. "No, there was no one in the parking lot, I'm sure of it. And I think I would have known if anyone else was still in the Center."

Gracie wished she could remember more. "I just can't believe anyone would steal that pitcher and bowl."

"There's always an explanation," Herb told her. "The question remains as to whether knowing it will make a difference to getting what's disappeared back again!"

Gracie barely had had time to finish putting away her groceries when Marge, along with Comfort Harding, appeared at the back door.

"Smells delicious," Comfort said, following Marge to the kitchen table.

"Blueberry buckle," Gracie identified the scent for her.

"I made it earlier this morning and I can see Uncle Miltie's had a second helping while I was at the store."

Marge, making herself at home, selected mugs from the cupboard. "Where is the darling old codger, anyway?"

"It's his day to do the morning story time at the library. My dear uncle," Gracie told Comfort, "as you well know, fancies himself a comedian, but I think he actually gets a lot of his material from the preschool set!"

"Lillian is always looking for jokes to exchange with Uncle Miltie, that's for sure," Comfort said.

Gracie cut them each a piece of the blueberry buckle, as Marge explained that Comfort had the day off and had dropped by her place with examples of her creative handiwork.

"Marge has graciously offered to take some of my quilts

on consignment," Comfort explained. "That is, mine plus several others from women in my quilting club."

The stock in Marge's little gift shop was charmingly eclectic. And always chosen with her personal touch. It included everything from greeting cards to fashion accessories.

"I stopped in the other day looking for a gift to send my sister," Comfort went on, "and noticed a handmade patchwork vest. Marge and I got to talking about quilts—"

"Comfort's work is beautiful!" Marge interjected, while taking milk from the refrigerator. "Who would imagine one of you math and science types being so artistic?" She smiled at the young mother. "A nurse anesthetist who can quilt."

"You're going to have to stop in and see her Mariner's Compass design," Marge told Gracie, then turned to Comfort. "I have just the place to display it."

Marge took the chair next to Gracie. "And you better stop by soon, because as pretty as it is, that quilt won't remain in my shop for long. It's museum quality!"

A blush tinged Comfort's lovely brown complexion. Her modesty made Gracie smile. Rick, her husband, was a fortunate man—and he, equally, was a favorite of Gracie's.

Arlen and Wendy would like them, she knew, and her frequent prayer was for friends like these for her son and his wife. Living in New York, they were so busy with their careers—but she longed for them to discover what the Hardings had realized: that making time for themselves and giving to a community were key ingredients for a happy life.

"Comfort has suggested creating a quilt that will commemorate our history. Eternal Hope's, I mean. Doesn't that sound like a great idea?"

"I saw it in a quilting magazine. There was a photo of a gorgeous one that a church in Pennsylvania had made, and it featured squares created by many of the member families. It was . . . splendid. An achievement to admire and be inspired by."

"We could have a good old-fashioned quilting bee!" Marge suddenly burst out. "Wow! It just occurred to me!"

Gracie agreed it sounded like a wonderful idea. After all, many of their congregation loved handicraft projects. And there were many talented seamstresses, she knew. "We could discuss it at choir practice." She had almost forgotten! "I told Barb that I'd help her pick out music for Founders Sunday in Fairweather Park."

"We're really looking forward to the community worship service," Comfort told her. "When Rick heard about the old-fashioned Sunday School picnic and relay games, he started practicing with Lillian for the three-legged race."

Marge chuckled. "What a father-daughter duo that will be! I can just picture little bitty Lillian strapped to that big lug of a husband of yours. She can hang on just about knee-high."

Comfort looked amused at the thought, too. "Moving to Willow Bend has been like a dream come true for our family."

She confessed, "I was against the move at first. I'm a city girl—an Easterner at heart, or so I thought."

Rick, with his choir duties and many volunteer activities, fit into the community and church family easily. For Comfort, finding her place had a been a little harder, since she worked such long hours at the hospital. Gracie was happy now to see her so enthusiastic about the Founders Day Celebration and the church.

"There's even going to be an old-fashioned tent meeting that evening," Marge told Comfort. "Maybe Rick told you that all the choirs in town have been invited. And that he's been asked to sing a solo."

"That's the concert for which I promised to look at music." Gracie smiled at her friend. "You're not the only one, Marge, who forgets to write things down."

"I can let you have a good planner," Marge grinned. "Barely used."

This provided the perfect opening for discussing what was really on Gracie's mind, so she told them about the mysterious theft. "Somebody must have slipped in while we were hauling stuff, Marge. Could it have been possible?"

"I didn't see anybody."

"Anyway, Herb's going to want to talk to us. I called him on his cell phone earlier, but I'm sure he'll have more questions. I'm praying the pitcher and bowl turn up. We're honest folks around here, so there's got to be an explanation. But until it's found, let's concentrate on the present: the quilt. I love your idea."

"I'd be willing to work with the congregation," Comfort said, "to help anyone design a square. Possibly I could even do the work for those unable to do it themselves."

Marge rubbed her hands together. "We'll have to get started right away, if we want a quilt by Founders Day!"

Comfort beamed.

Thank You, Lord, for giving us this opportunity to draw another shy lamb closer to the center of the fold.

"We could ask Marybeth to bring her heirloom quilt to church," Gracie suggested. "She could share its history as a way of inspiring people. When you see it, you really understand how fabric can be a medium for preserving the present for the future, even if quilts originally were made for practical purposes."

"Oh, this is exciting!" Marge said. "I can hardly wait to see how it all unfolds. Just like a quilt! Get it?"

"I think Uncle Miltie might be rubbing off a bit on you, my dear. Watch out!" Gracie told her friend drily.

After Marge and Comfort had left, Gracie began doodling on the pad with the notes from her conversation with Herb.

Uncle Miltie materialized at her shoulder. "What's up? You look too serious."

She explained about their pastor's phone call. Uncle Miltie listened carefully. Not a day went by that she didn't thank God for bringing them together. Dora, her aunt and Uncle Miltie's wife, had died shortly after El was killed. Because of his physical difficulties, a temporary move to Willow Bend made sense for Uncle Miltie at the time. But what had begun as a temporary living arrangement had become a comfortable companionship.

As Gracie filled him in on the morning, Gooseberry leaped into her lap, curling himself into a ball. She stroked his soft pumpkin-colored fur. The loud purr he began emitting was familiar background music to her sorting out of thoughts.

"You talk to Rocky yet?" Uncle Miltie wanted to know.

She shook her head, realizing how natural asking for advice from the editor had become. Uncle Miltie was as fond of Rocco Gravino as she was, even if they enjoyed sparring with one another.

"Think he's still in his office?" she wondered out loud.

"Won't know until you call him."

"What a pundit!"

"More like a fun-dit!" He chuckled. "Hey, that reminds me of a story I heard today. There were these four guys, see, Everybody, Somebody, Anybody and Nobody."

He paused. Gracie raised an eyebrow. He continued, "There was an important job to be done and Everybody was sure that Somebody would do it. Anybody could have done it, but Nobody did. Somebody got angry about this, because it was Everybody's job. Everybody thought Anybody could do it, but Nobody realized that Everybody wouldn't do it. It ended up that Everybody blamed Somebody when Nobody did what Anybody could have done."

Uncle Miltie flashed a satisfied grin. "Call Gravino. We might not be Everybody, but we are Somebody. Maybe we can figure something out. Anyway, I bet you he's probably up for a mug of your coffee."

Rocky arrived about a half hour later. "Any dunkers? You know me—always prefer it with a few crumbs floating in it."

She poured his coffee. "I saw Sue and Mike at the reception," Gracie said, following his lead in small talk. "Mike says you all have really been busy."

"What else is new?" Rocky eyed her over his mug. "And don't mention Cordelia Fountain wanting a story, since that's not news, either."

They grinned at one another.

"Actually, now she doesn't. She phoned in the news this morning about the theft. She had the scoop before my reporters, so it was a good thing I didn't dodge her, as I usually do."

Gracie explained that Cordelia was the first to the scene of the crime because they were to pack up the exhibit.

"Anyway, she wants me to hold the story for fear it will deter folks from lending their family possessions to the exhibit." Rocky put his mug down. "Cordelia is positive the thief is someone from Avery. She's convinced they're trying to throw a wrench in our celebration plans."

He crossed his arms and leaned back in the chair. "She reminded me that Willow Bend is the oldest town in the county by default. And according to her, the good citizens of Avery have been nursing a grudge ever since. I knew there'd always been some rivalry between the two towns, but it seemed friendly enough to me."

"So someone from Avery is our thief?" Uncle Miltie asked.

Rocky shrugged. "That's just Cordelia's theory."

"Well, you know how fraternities try to sneak over and steal the mascot from another. Next thing you know, the rival one has to strike back. Usually it ends with everybody happy, though. At least that's how they show it on television."

Gracie looked at Rocky, hoping he'd offer a more serious scenario as a possibility.

"It turns out that pitcher and bowl are worth at least several thousand dollars. Can you believe it! Your pastor is pressing me not to do a story, either, because Carl Jackson is threatening to name Eternal Hope as codefendant in a lawsuit."

Rocky shook his head. "Nobody wants me to write the biggest story Willow Bend has had in a long time!"

He eyed Gracie. "That's the one thing I don't like about living in a small town. You all pull rank, seeming to think your subscription entitles you to a place on my board of directors. That is, if I had one. Not to mention Cordelia's delusion that she's our main benefactor with *four*—not just one, mind you," he said, imitating their local grand dame, "but four subscriptions to 'your poorly managed *Mason County Gazette.*'"

Gracie felt guilty for hoping, as well, that Rocky would hold the story. She simply wasn't yet convinced it really was robbery. She still held out hope. "It could all be some kind of mistake, one we just haven't figured out yet. Can't you allow some time to let the person responsible come forward before you call it a crime?"

"I hate to burst your Pollyanna bubble, Gracie, but it already is a crime. Choosing the wrong color paint is a mistake; walking out of a church with a valuable heirloom is illegal! I don't care what the motives were."

He softened. "But yes, I've promised to hold the story. It seems you, Cordelia, Herb and Paul Meyer were all poured from the same mold."

"Maybe instead of being poured, we're being molded," Gracie said, seizing the opportunity. What she meant to convey was that it was again a moment when her cynical friend might reconsider his spiritual stubbornness.

Rocky ignored the meaning implicit in her response. "I suppose we should make a suspect list now. I told Herb we'd talk to people." He flashed a roguish grin. "Discreetly, of course."

Gracie retrieved her pad. "Marge and I were the last ones in the church. Paul and Cordelia left just before we did, but that was a long time after everyone else was gone. I figure we have about an hour to account for, and so I was trying to remember everyone who'd been in the building toward the end."

She handed him the list. "They're almost all church members, folks who stayed around to help tidy up before leaving. And I can vouch for every one of them."

"... Pastor Paul, Cordelia Fountain, Marge Lawrence, Barb Jennings, Roy Bell, Ed Larson, and Bert Benton, saints one and all," he said, reading the list. "If you don't mind, we won't completely eliminate them—not until after we talk to them, anyway."

She ignored his implication that there was no guarantee, ever, than anyone was perfectly trustworthy and above suspicion. Of course, that was true, but these were her friends. "I should have put myself on that list. I was the last one out."

"There could have been somebody hiding, waiting for the opportunity to filch the set," Uncle Miltie suggested.

"Nope, no one," she told them. "I'm sure of it."

"What makes you so sure?" Rocky asked.

She really didn't know. "A feeling. You just always know when you're not alone—you can sense the presence of another person."

"Gracie's intuition." Rocky wrote the word on the pad and underlined it.

"A lot of cases are solved on hunches," Uncle Miltie said, "and Gracie's are pretty shrewd a lot of the time, if you ask me."

"She does have a sixth sense for teasing out a detail we all overlooked," Rocky conceded. "But I'm not convinced one of these saints didn't stay behind and conceal himself until after you and Marge left. They know the layout of the place, that's for sure. Familiarity might have tripped your intuition, Gracie, my girl."

She had to admit that that *was* a possibility.

"The other angle is that it was a setup," Uncle Miltie suggested. "There's the possibility Carl Jackson took it for the insurance money. I've seen that on TV, too."

"That thought also crossed my mind," Gracie admitted. "I don't know the Jacksons very well. . . ."

"Many a saint is seduced by money," Rocky reminded her.

Granted every saint could have a tainted past and, granted, everyone is a sinner. But saints had been forgiven, and they were all sinners with a future—a bright future. That future, she determined, was the best deterrent to sin. But could her friend ever appreciate her logic?

"That's probably true," she conceded. "Sadly, money does inspire most crimes. And who would have known the value of that heirloom better than the Jacksons?"

Rocky nodded. "My point, precisely. The problem is Carl is out of town, and Deborah seems too timid."

Uncle Miltie scratched his head. "Baffling, all right."

"Well, we have to start some place," Rocky was businesslike. "And since Gracie vouches for the Eternal Hope saints, I guess our first suspect is Mrs. Jackson."

He looked at her. "Then, Gracie, we've got Mrs. Fountain. I leave her to you. You're on your own with Willow Bend's redoubtable dowager!"

Gracie couldn't help needling him. "A big city tough guy like you intimidated by an elderly small town belle?"

"The belle is a bully! Or should I say bulldozer?"

They all laughed at the truth in that!

WHEN GRACIE AND ROCKY knocked at the Jacksons' door, Deborah appeared reluctant at first to let them in. After finally inviting them to come and sit down, she still seemed strained. She took them into an impeccably furnished parlor, the eerily hollow ticking of several clocks making an already cool atmosphere seem glacial.

Gracie sat on the red velvet sofa and glanced around at the gold leaf frames, velvet drapes and crystal chandeliers. The simple, sturdy pitcher and bowl definitely had not been on display in this room of the house.

Deborah stood watching her from behind a brocade wing chair, further indication they should keep their visit short and sweet.

"You have a lovely home," she told the woman.

Deborah accepted the compliment but didn't look any happier. "Most of the furnishings I inherited from my great-aunt, whom I think you must have known." She rubbed her hand across the nap of the chair, much like a child would a security blanket, and her gaze roamed from ceiling to windows, rarely pausing on her guests. "I love these things because they belonged to her. Each one has a story behind it."

Gracie said, "I only knew her to nod at. But I've long admired the house. The furnishings are elegant—so many antiques!"

Deborah's gray eyes were guarded. "Carl is the one who knows antiques." Her lips set in a tight line.

She went on, "Aunt Aggie and I bought that chair you're sitting in at an auction here in Willow Bend when I was little. I wanted a special place to read when I visited." She pointed to the French doors beside Gracie. "That was my favorite spot."

They all looked out to the garden beyond.

Deborah changed the subject. "When we first found the pitcher and bowl in the carriage house, Carl recognized their value. He's a history buff, particularly when it comes to the Civil War."

"I'll bet he liked Howie Anderson's Confederate rifle." Rocky shot Gracie a furtive look. "I know I was quite impressed by it."

"No, being interested in the war and its history doesn't necessarily mean he's a gun buff. In fact, he never even let our son have a water pistol. He likes books, letters—that type of war memorabilia."

She eyed Rocky. "What you really want to know is if my husband was at the reception. That's why you asked about the rifle, isn't it? Well, no, Mr. Gravino, he was not at the reception. As I've already told the police, Carl has been in Chicago on business the last few days. I called him there from the church."

"But you have to admit," Rocky pressed her, "it does seem more than coincidence that your husband insured these belongings just weeks before a theft."

"Not really, considering that he'd just watched a show on television, where they assessed a similar piece. We were both surprised at the value."

Gracie searched her mind for some subject to ease the strain, but Rocky kept control of the conversation. "Can you provide me with the name of the appraiser you then went to? I want to get the facts straight before I write the story."

"Carl will have to do that. He'll be home tonight."

Gracie now broke in. "I've noticed your lovely greenhouse when I've been out walking. I've often hoped to stop and chat and tell you how beautiful your flowers are."

A slight smile. "Thanks. With my odd hours at the hospital, I don't have much time to socialize. I love my garden in the early morning and evening. Things smell sweeter, and the shadows are softer. It's so peaceful."

"A nice habit," Gracie told her. "I often get distracted and so I miss those spectacular times of day. But they are blessed moments, I agree."

Deborah's expression softened momentarily. "It pains me that we're in this position. We lent the pitcher and bowl to the Founders Day Celebration Committee in good faith, and we harbor no animosity to you, the church, or the town, for that matter. We only want to recoup what we've lost."

Deborah met Gracie's gaze. "I would have liked to have met you under better circumstances. I've heard so many nice things about you."

Gracie could feel the woman's regret. *Lord, help me see her as You do. I sense her loneliness. Open the way for us to be friends.*

"I, too, am sorry that this couldn't have been a social call," Gracie admitted. "But I'd still love to see your greenhouse and gardens sometime."

"I raise orchids." Her smile seemed genuine. "I'll be happy to give you one when you come to visit."

Deborah looked at Rocky. "I don't know what more I can say, since I gave a full account to the police chief. We signed a release lending the piece to the Historical Society for six weeks. Really, they assumed the risk. Please, why don't we let the insurance companies settle this?"

"As I understand it," Rocky said, "that piece of paper was simply a receipt for the loan. I don't believe anything was mentioned about responsibility for loss or theft. And I'm curious as to why your husband is threatening a lawsuit, since the set is insured."

She straightened. "Really, my husband handles these things. You'll have to talk to him. Now, unless you have further business, I have some gardening to do."

"*Brrr!*" Rocky said when they got outside. "I could have used earmuffs in there. Pretty frosty."

They walked to Rocky's little black sedan in silence. Gracie's own thoughts were on Carl. She could picture a small, balding, meticulously groomed man with wire-rimmed glasses, but the personality behind the appearance was less clear. She would have to meet Deborah's husband.

"What do we know about Carl Jackson?" Rocky asked her, as they fastened their seat belts.

Gracie laughed. "You must have been reading my mind. I honestly don't know anything about the man, but there's something off plumb here, as Miltie would say, and I can't put my finger on it . . ."

"Your sleuth sense!"

"Oh, I know you like to tease me, but I'm no Nancy Drew or Miss Marple! Sometimes I get lucky, but it's only because I care so much about everything being right with all my friends and neighbors! Trouble isn't fun!" She was suddenly serious.

"Gracie," Rocky matched her now in seriousness, "all I know is that there's a light emanating from you that warms people, even that chilly lady we just talked to. Maybe you draw the power from your faith—to illuminate dark places. What's certain is how special you are and how you so often see what others don't."

She was touched by his belief in her.

"So my soul-sleuther, what do you think is really going on in that house? My hunch is that Carl set the whole thing up for an insurance scam. I've never met the man, but already I don't like him."

She looked his way and he chuckled. "I know you, Gracie Parks, right now you're probably praying for that woman and her husband. Don't think I didn't notice; the colder she got, the warmer you seemed. I'm sure you meant it when you told her that you wanted to see those orchids."

Her "of course" was playful. Rocky was always a challenge to her, especially because he was so quick to catch inconsistencies in people.

"You do agree, don't you, that Deborah is hiding something? Carl is our prime suspect—Herb thinks the same—but we just can't put him at the scene of the crime. Whatever I think about his wife, I can't picture her having the nerve to sneak in and steal that pitcher and bowl."

Gracie agreed. "Also, I suspect she may not be as fully supportive of her husband as her words imply."

Rocky shot her a glance that invited her to continue.

"Did you notice her left hand?"

"She wasn't wearing a wedding ring. Lots of folks don't."

"Women *always* do."

Rocky seemed to ponder that fact. "So, you think she may not be happily married? Maybe she'd talk more candidly to a friend."

"Perhaps."

"When did you say you were going to go see her orchids?"

She shot him a furtive look. "I didn't."

"How about giving Herb a call on my cell phone?" Rocky hastily changed the subject. "Let's see what he's turned up on the case."

What he'd turned up, Gracie found, were headaches: a string of them. There had been a dozen calls from nervous owners of antiques lent for the exhibit, and there'd been a fax from the insurance investigator, and the rest of the town seemed to want to play a Twenty Questions round for which he didn't have the answers.

"Almost everyone he interviewed has a theory on who took the set. Cordelia Fountain and Pastor Paul have even been implicated. Can you imagine?"

"Sounds like the rumor-mongers have the real scoop." Rocky glanced her way. "What is it they say about the church grapevine? Makes for pretty sour sacrament, if you ask me."

Gracie decided not to comment.

"That was a cheap shot." He glanced her way again. "I am sorry, Gracie."

"Forgiven."

"I really envy your faith. Its meaning is so obviously greater than life itself for you."

She nodded, but didn't say anything. *Lord, speak to his heart, meet him in his deepest longing. Help him to recognize that the grounding he senses in me is really You.*

Gracie kept her gaze on his profile and her heart open to the Lord's leading.

"Don't get me wrong," he continued. "It's not that I don't believe. I'm no atheist . . . maybe I'm just scared cynical."

She smiled, silently encouraging him to continue.

"Church doesn't fit right." Another glance her way. "You know what I mean?"

Focusing back on the road, he was quiet for a few moments. Then, with one hand on the steering wheel, he tugged at his already unbuttoned collar. "You put on a tie to make yourself presentable, but you can't wait to pop that button—loosen the noose. Church is like that for me. I've got to breathe."

Gracie smiled with God.

Rocky pulled in behind Charlie Harris at the Willow Mart. His vehicle was a bicycle converted into a makeshift pickup, with a plywood cab connected to a wooden cart mounted on two wheels. It was quite ingenious, really, Gracie concluded. It also saved money on registrations, inspections and licensing.

"I have to pick up some dog food or the boys are going to eat *me*," Rocky said, referring to the basset hound he called Rover and Gent, a sweet little cocker spaniel.

"I'll wait here."

He headed into the store as Charlie appeared carrying a paper bag. It occurred to Gracie to mention to him the project Comfort had in mind. After all, over the years, he could be seen most Sundays at early and late services, enjoying the music—slipping away, however, before anyone else.

"Meemaw would have liked that," Charlie told her after she explained. "My grandma loved to remember the old times. She was the best storyteller. I can tell that lady Meemaw's story. Sure, I can do that."

Gracie made small talk as she waited for Rocky, enjoying the gentle nature of her companion. When she complimented Charlie on his bicycle's originality, he grinned. "I don't like cars much," he told her.

"They go too fast—scare me. Too many accidents." He paused. "Horses was nice. You remember when we had horses in Willow Bend?"

She shook her head, although she did recall visits to her grandparents' Indiana farm. "My grandfather had a work horse," she told him. "He wore blinders when he pulled the hay cart. He couldn't see you coming, but he always knew you were there. He would turn his head to greet me, no matter how sneaky I tried to be."

"Yeah, horses is smart. Weren't nearly so many accidents when horses was doing the driving." He punctuated that recollection with a firm shake of the head.

"Hey, Charlie!" Rocky was back.

She glanced between the two. "You two know each other?"

"Charlie recycles our aluminum cans and bottles." Rocky told her. "I figure he's probably made a million or two off of us by now."

Charlie excused himself, saying Miss Cordelia was waiting dinner for him. "She told me to bring a loaf of bread. I got two of 'em, figuring she'd need another one tomorrow."

"That's good thinking," Rocky said. "If half a loaf is better than none, then two's got to be *even* better!"

Charlie mounted the seat of his converted bicycle. "You folks have a nice evening, now, hear?" He waved.

"You too, Charlie." Gracie raised her hand in return.

Rocky opened his passenger door. "Madam."

"Thank you, kind sir."

After they got back under way, Gracie asked, "What do you know about Charlie Harris?"

"He's rich." Rocky shot her a wily grin. "You thinking of marrying for money?"

She ignored his teasing. "What do you mean?" she demanded to know. "How do you know that?"

"We journalists have our ways."

"Please!"

"Truthfully, if you need information, just listen to bank tellers and switchboard operators. They know what's going on! Charlie happened to be in front of me in line one day, and when he left, I made a joke about him being a millionaire. Vivian Traub couldn't resist telling me I wasn't too far off. His grandmother left him a bundle, it seems, and though the teller was too professional to put a figure to his wealth, I got the distinct impression there were a few more zeroes at the end than my account shows."

That was a surprise! Gracie found herself startled into silence, as she contemplated what an unlikely plutocrat Charlie looked to be, with his faded overalls and mended shirts.

"Yup. Not all of it is in cash, though," Rocky continued. "I guess his grandmother made a few good investments. He's also given quite a bit away over the years. Anyway, that's what Vivian gave me to believe, as cagey as she tried to be."

Charlie was signaling with his arm to make a left turn.

"A peculiar philanthropist."

Rocky looked her way again. "So, what's for supper?"

She laughed. "Haven't I heard that line before?"

"Most weeks," he agreed. "I figured you'd feed me and then we'd go over the facts, maybe pick up the thread that will unravel the mystery."

"We're having Yankee pot roast."

"How about some of those spiced peaches of yours?"

"Only if you help Uncle Miltie put up the new curtain rods in the guest room."

"Deal!"

Gracie suddenly spied Chuckie Moon and his pals loitering in front of The Sweet Shoppe. "Could you pull over for a minute? I've got a project I want to talk to the boys about."

She closed the car door. "I'll be right back."

"Wow, aren't you dapper!" Gracie looked Chuckie up and down. His blonde hair was neatly trimmed—a handsome relief from the bright green spike he'd been sporting. He also had on a sweater and khakis, another surprise in the sartorial department. "What's with the new look?"

"He's gone preppy," his friend Quasi explained.

Gracie crossed her arms and did a double take. "I don't miss the grunge. You are one handsome fellow, Charles Moon."

He flushed.

"Chuck is looking at colleges," Martin told her. "So he's got to look the part if he's going to get all those scholarships. He's a brainiac, you know."

Quasi snickered. "If they ask him one of the questions on a cereal box, that is."

Chuckie scowled.

"Seriously!" Quasi elbowed Chuckie. "He's ten times smarter than us. And he's going to share his first million with the only guys who would put up with his weirdness!"

She knew the boy was smart. He had always just needed a shot of self-confidence. She sent a thank-you heavenward for the new spirit she sensed in him. Then she turned to Martin. "What are you going to do when you graduate?"

"State police. If I get accepted, that is."

"The guy's a moron," Quasi told her. "Perfect candidate."

Gracie eyed Quasi, to let him know she didn't appreciate his jab at a profession comprised of indispensable community servants. Martin followed her cue and poked his friend.

"Me, I'm outta here the day after I graduate," Quasi announced. "Timothy Weaver is California-bound. Figure I'll bum around for a while, get out of my grandma's hair. I hear they've got some awesome half-pipe skateboarding ramps out there."

Gracie chatted a couple of minutes, then tried out on them her idea of helping Cordelia clean up her cellar.

"No way! I'm not gonna help that old witch!" Quasi shook his head. "Not even if I was trapped in an elevator with her and her burning broom."

Martin objected, "She's not so bad."

"We egged her on," Chuckie admitted. "Remember how we used to fool around in back of her place just to get a rise out of her?"

The other two looked sheepish.

"We've been pretty crummy to that old lady," Chuckie told

Gracie. "So I don't mind trying to make up for it. Pay our dues."

"Come on, admit it," Martin coaxed. "You enjoyed hassling her, too, man. She was pretty funny. Remember her? Chasing after us with that broom of hers, yelling 'Shoo, shoo, you hooligans!'"

Quasi laughed. "Yeah, for a while I actually believed she *was* a witch, with that black cat and all."

Gracie tried to hide her smile.

"No, seriously, Mrs. Parks, witches can look as normal as you and me."

Now that was funny, considering Quasi not only had a nose ring, but several tattoos. His pants were six sizes too big, and a chain hung down almost to his brand-name sneakers. His tee shirt was ripped and pinned, and he had a wisp of hair hanging off his chin.

Chuckie groaned.

"Quasi, *you're* the moron," Martin told him.

"We'll do the work, " Chuckie told her. "You've been fair with us. It's the least we can do. We'll do it for you." He looked to the other two for approval.

Nods all around.

"Who knows," Martin said, making a motion in Quasi's direction, "we might even find out he's right and dig up something weird in the basement—creep city!"

Quasi grinned. "Maybe there'll be a bottle with a genie. Chuck gets to go to college, Martin gets a super sporty police cruiser, and the hottest babe on the beach falls for yours truly."

"Well, I doubt that's the kind of relic you'll find, if any, amidst all the debris. I'll talk to Mrs. Fountain—but, Chuckie, you should go over and explain, as well, that we've had this conversation." She turned to walk back to Rocky's car, then added, "And it wouldn't hurt to check with Pastor Paul. You might even get some of the Youth Group to help you. Extra hands, you know."

Silently, she sent a prayer ahead. *Please, Lord, oversee this venture. Don't let them do something too stupid, something that might spoil this opportunity to change Cordelia's opinion of them while serving also to draw them into the fold.*

"*Hmm?*" Rocky was standing by the car, watching her.

"A God thing."

He smiled affectionately. "Say no more."

4

GRACIE HAD OFTEN WONDERED if the devil hadn't invented committees to confound the work of the Kingdom. Certainly, Eternal Hope's newest one seemed to fit the description. Pastor Paul had received an anonymous cash gift for the purchase of new choir robes. He was hoping a decision might be made in time to have them for the choir's performance on Founders Sunday. But definite problems had arisen when it came to selecting color and style. Disagreement reigned.

Although the choir's meeting to choose robes had been launched in enthusiasm, it finished in discouraging fashion. Gracie had also wanted to discuss Comfort's idea for cooperatively creating a quilt, imagining it would be a pleasant diversion from the robes dispute—but it turned out her friends found the idea too daunting a project.

Comfort, who had come to help explain the details, remained quiet. When it was apparent the meeting was getting nowhere, Marge called for a refreshment break. Gracie made her way to the kitchen by herself.

They had come to choir practice together and stayed for the meeting afterward about the robes. On the way over, Gracie's mind had been on the theft and the mystery surrounding it, so Marge, ever obliging, had given her the space she needed to think. She had just popped in a cassette of Celtic hymns, and told Gracie to relax. As always, Gracie appreciated how well her friend knew her.

Now she unsnapped the plastic container to take one of the chocolate-chip cookies Marybeth had brought. Delicious! Gracie had read that some cultures considered the stomach the center of emotion. She chuckled at the thought of a lacy paper facsimile of that organ on Valentine's Day. But she also knew a bite of chocolate would make her mood improve.

She could hear two of her friends discussing the quilt idea. Marge was suggesting that they enjoy the cookies, instead, and talk about less stressful things. Gracie was proud of her friend's diplomacy.

Sharing food had a way of bringing people together. No wonder common meals were so important to the first Christians. *Agape* dinners, she remembered Pastor Paul calling them. Yes, offering her catering skills was a very appropriate way to serve her church. She sensed God's quiet approval. He was there, lending silent support. Marge's model was the right one. True friends!

Thank You, Lord, for putting my mind at ease. In a kitchen where I'm so at home, You always seem to be, too.

The Turner twins suddenly appeared.

"I love Comfort's idea of making a quilt," Tyne told Gracie.

Tish nodded. "It's a wonderful way to express what Eternal Hope means to many of us."

"Forget that," her sister joked. "We should just offer it as a wedding gift to any woman who will marry our good-looking pastor!"

They both laughed.

Gracie could only shake her head.

"Don't worry, Gracie," Tish said. She understood her friend's concern over the way the meeting had gone. "And don't fret about the squabbling. We'll make a decision—you know we always do. A few cookies, a cup of tea and before you know it, it'll all be fine. When we leave here today, we'll not only have the choir robes picked, but a bunch of commitments for that quilt. That's what I love about us—we can agree to disagree, and still remain good friends."

"I guess Eternal Hope isn't called that for no reason!" Marge suddenly appeared and quipped.

"I hear that gun of your father-in-law's is quite valuable." Gracie now said to Tyne, changing the course of the conversation. "Does he have it insured?"

Tyne furrowed her brow. "I'm not sure. Probably not, knowing Dad. But I don't suppose it matters all that much to him, because he didn't pay anything for it. He found it when they cleared away that old foundation to build their new cabin. It has a nice wooden box, but he prefers to display it above the fireplace at home.

"Mother Anderson would love to see that gun disappear. She hates it hanging there in the family room, and would like it relegated to the cabin. But Dad won't hear of it."

"Maybe he *should* have it insured, after what happened," Tish told her sister. "I'm glad they've finally locked all those mementos and treasures in a display case at the library. They probably should have been there in the first place, even if I, for one, felt honored to have the initial exhibition here at Eternal Hope."

Gracie set the teakettle on the stove.

"As much as we hate to face it," Tyne said, "there are always going to be dishonest people, even in Willow Bend." She made a face.

Tish sighed.

As they rejoined their fellow choir members. Gracie overheard Barb Jennings sharing Cordelia's theory that the rivalry between Avery and Willow Bend might be the motive behind the theft. Estelle Livett dismissed that idea as ridiculous. Barb insisted it wasn't impossible—even if it was improbable—and Marge stepped in to mediate.

These were good friends, and usually all agreeable folks. Gracie knew them well and forgave them their shortcomings as they forgave hers. And why shouldn't there be cantankerous moments? Like any family, the Eternal Hope choir was as frustrating at times as it was cherished by them all.

"So, who do you think is our magnanimous donor?" Marge asked, "Choir robes for all of us? That's a hefty gift! We don't know that many folks who do that without expecting at least a thank-you!"

Marybeth overheard them, "I figure it's someone elderly. A member who wants to do something nice before he or she dies. We actually have quite a few well-to-do seniors." Marge looked skeptical.

"The important thing is that we make a decision. I'm sure our benefactor didn't intend so much discord. Let's try to make a decision—for the giver's sake!" Gracie thought this line of reasoning might help.

Marybeth confessed, "I'm guilty of wanting my own way. I think those sky-blue gowns would look elegant against the dark wood of the loft. Like heaven and earth. But you're right, Gracie. Such a windfall is a blessing for all of us, and harmony isn't only about music."

Gracie excused herself to go confer with Comfort, who was still seated at the edge of the group, listening. "I thought your idea for a church quilt was wonderful."

"It's a big undertaking. I understand that."

"I just wanted to tell you that I appreciate your patience. But you seem to understand the dynamics here." Gracie smiled at her.

"It comes with practice. I am the mother of a preschooler!"

"Ah, that explains it!"

"Seriously, Gracie, it's not a problem. It doesn't matter to me if we choose another project. I'm just happy to be involved in the Founders Day events at any level."

"And choosing new choir robes?"

Comfort laughed. "I think it's a good idea none of the guys chose to stay for the discussion."

Gracie had to agree.

Comfort smiled. "And, Gracie, you don't have to apologize for our sisters in Christ. Remember what Pastor Paul says. 'Church is not a hotel for saints, but a hospital for sinners.' We're all in this together."

Gracie had only one thing to say: "Amen."

"Listen, the Harding family feels at home at Eternal Hope. You've all been wonderful to us." Comfort shook her finger accusingly. "Although, Gracie, I must admit that I've felt a wee bit envious of my husband's enjoying all this fellowship. Until now, that is."

Now it was Gracie's turn to laugh.

But she turned more serious an instant later. "I've often told Arlen about you and Rick. I admire the way you seem to manage career and family together."

"I don't know how I could do it without Rick. I'm so thankful he likes pitching in when it comes to domestic chores."

"Your husband lights up like a power plant when he talks about you and Lillian."

Comfort leaned back. "Well, I need him. Sometimes, you know, I get caught up in my career and lose perspective. Then Rick pulls me back, reminding me that we definitely wanted to leave the city and its too-fast pace behind.

"When I have time off, I'm not allowed to wear a watch." She laughed. "Rick has even stooped to hiding the clocks when we're on vacation. If I ask him, 'What time is it?' You know what he says?"

Gracie was curious.

"He says, 'Time to enjoy life.' And I know he's right."

"My parents aren't churchgoers," Comfort confessed. "I love them dearly but have longed for mentors, Christians to encourage and guide Rick and me in our marriage and in our parenting. I can't tell you how much it has meant to call all of you family."

"Comfort, dear, we feel the same way."

Marybeth came over to them. "A compromise has come to mind, at least in the quilt debate. I want to hear what you think. What about family banners? Members can use needlepoint, embroidery, felt with glue, whatever, to create something to represent their faith story or family heritage.

"Our more ambitious members can help put together a quilt if they wish, but this way those who feel they don't have the time or talent to commit to quilting don't have to."

She looked at Comfort. "We'd love to have you on board for the quilt, once it's underway, that's for sure!"

Marge reminded them, "Now if we can just make a decision on the robes!"

"Robes!" Their embattled choir director was ready for another round. She tapped her baton on the table. "Come along, my friends, we have a decision to make."

Comfort and Marybeth continued to whisper about the two crafts projects, with Rick's wife volunteering her special sewing machine, and also the assistance of her quilting club, if needed.

"I love to sew," Marybeth exclaimed. "And I've always wanted to make a quilt, so I'll help you. I really feel inspired by my own family quilt."

Comfort was obviously pleased to have found someone with whom to share this special passion of hers. Her eyes sparkled.

"There's nothing we can't accomplish with prayer," Barb was saying. "Let's all just take a moment to put ourselves in the right frame of mind. We can make this decision tonight.

"Lord, help us to listen to one another and respect each other's opinions. We will be wearing these robes to sing Your praises, so we ask that You aid us as we make our choice of raiment."

"Now!" Barb continued. "We've got business to finish. Remember, choir practice starts and ends punctually! And this adjunct committee will do the same."

Marybeth sighed, "It's like being in school!"

"We know we need to be comfortable," Gracie now offered.

"The fabric has to breathe," Estelle pointed out.

Marge agreed. "And let's make sure it's an upbeat color."

"Anything but red," said Tish.

Tyne agreed. "We look terrible in red."

In less than fifteen minutes, they'd decided on ivory robes with interchangeable stoles in bright colors. Suddenly, as if no bickering had ever taken place, everyone was satisfied with the outcome and eager to get started on one of the sewing projects. Peace reigned.

For the moment, at any rate.

"Do you think Comfort and I might come over one morning to look at your family quilt?" Gracie asked Marybeth.

"There's no need. I have it with me, in a cedar box in my car."

They followed her to the parking lot. She opened her trunk and then unfastened the catch to the slender wooden container. As she pulled out the quilt, they saw how its colors had faded to softer shades that were nonetheless still vibrant.

Gracie thought the workmanship extraordinary, and Comfort agreed. She stood back to take in the whole effect.

Gracie moved closer, lifting the corner of the quilt to examine the stitches. "Beautiful!"

Comfort rubbed her hand over the quilt top, her expression somber. Gracie had noticed while Marybeth was talking, Comfort seemed to be distracted.

"Is something wrong?" Gracie asked. Marybeth looked on curiously. Then Barb, getting into her car, called out for a hand and Marybeth moved off obligingly to help her.

Comfort shook her head.

Gracie moved closer to her friend, hoping she'd share what was was on her mind.

Comfort continued caressing the knotted nubs on the quilt top. Her touch was almost reverent.

"It's beautiful, isn't it?"

"*Umm, hmm,*" Comfort acknowledged, seemingly unable to speak.

Then, her eyes brimming with tears, Comfort revealed what she was thinking. Her voice caught as she somberly told Gracie, "A white woman did not create this quilt. . . ."

5

GRACIE STARED AT COMFORT.

"All that I see here tells me that is a slave quilt." The African American woman spoke slowly. "And it is not just any slave quilt. This one's a true treasure, a piece of our past. Fabric and spirit, stitched in hope."

Gracie was uncertain. "I see how moved you are, but, please, you have to help me understand."

"See the knotting on the quilt top?" Comfort asked softly. "No white woman would have created such shoddy workmanship."

Gracie felt herself draw back.

"No, Gracie, I didn't mean that as an insult. Most domestic quilts feature tiny stitching. Slave ones, however, used heavy thread—sometimes even hemp, because it was more noticeable. The knots were tied in a scaled square of five- or ten-mil increments."

Comfort rubbed a knot between her fingers. "These seem unsightly but they are not defects and they were explained away to inquisitive masters as the effect of the uneven batting the slave was forced to use.

"However . . . this quilt was created with painstaking deliberation, with as much care and love as the finest European style they sought to duplicate.

"What's not widely known but is vital a part of our history is that these knots are part of a code, with the quilt itself a mnemonic device. Stitching, knotting, pattern, color—all work together to give information: miles, dates, places, lunar seasons—clues only the slaves recognized. The code was even transmitted through songs, as well. It was all part of the same goal, the same objective."

Comfort pointed to the squares. "These were maps to freedom, Gracie. Blazons to be hung on a fence, out a window, or over a clothesline. I've never seen one up close, although I've read about them in books. They're such noble relics!"

She went on. "Our family tradition has it that a quilt like this helped my great-great-grandmother escape to Rochester, New York, where she worked with Frederick Douglass."

"Along the Underground Railroad?" Gracie knew quilt designs: Monkey Wrench, North Star, Log Cabin, Shoofly, and Flying Geese. All were so familiar, yet she had never imagined the possibility that a quilt could be sending a message.

"Indeed," Comfort answered. "A story told in stitching

and pattern—and this one seems like it could be very much like the one that unfolded the path to freedom for my great-great-grandmother."

Comfort leaned close. "But let's keep my thoughts just between you and me. I can't be certain until I do some research."

Marybeth was now back beside them. "Exquisite, isn't it? Imagine the time Velina Ames spent creating it!"

"May I take a photograph of the quilt?" Comfort shot Gracie a glance. "I just happen to have a camera with me. I'd love to show a picture of it to my quilting class."

"You have a camera with you?"

"I carry around one of those little ones just in case Lillian does something especially cute. Candid shots are my favorites, so I like to be prepared."

Smiling outwardly, Gracie felt her insides tighten. Two histories, two stories. Two women caught in a potential conflict of interpretation and attribution. Fine when it was happening somewhere far away in a museum, Gracie thought to herself. But this was right here, in Willow Bend, and these were her friends.

Gracie beat the eggs with the ferocity of her confusion. She'd hoped baking would take her mind off a trio of upsetting telephone calls. For one, Herb Bower had no new leads on the disappearance of the pitcher and bowl.

Plus, it now looked like the Jacksons were, in fact, going through with a suit against the town of Willow Bend and Eternal Hope Community Church. Pastor Paul had heard the grim news, and he'd called Gracie.

Finally, the situation of the encrypted quilt came to mind. Comfort, she'd learned, had already contacted someone in Ohio, a historian who was ready to come right away to inspect Marybeth's quilt. It seemed to fit the documented descriptions perfectly, and though researchers were sure Underground Railroad quilts existed, few unchallenged examples had survived. Comfort had telephoned Gracie asking how best to broach the subject to Marybeth.

"Slow down, girl," suddenly came the voice of reason. Marge handed her the sugar. "That's cake batter, not meringue."

Gracie stopped mid-stroke. "My brain is churning faster than this egg beater! This whole business has me feeling totally at sea, and in a whirlpool, to boot. Did you know Herb has talked to the insurance investigator, who says Carl Jackson is claiming the pitcher and bowl were actually under-appraised? He intends to collect the remainder of the full value from the town and Eternal Hope."

Marge stared incredulously and Gracie continued. "He claims he had a newer informal evaluation at one of those antique road shows, but never bothered to change the policy. The company is refusing to pay until they've conducted a formal investigation. Believe it or not, Cordelia signed an affidavit as to the value of the set."

"What's going on? There was a time when you could leave your doors unlocked in Willow Bend! Now you can't even trust your neighbors not to march off to war with your enemy!"

Gracie now told her friend, "Okay, but I'm not going to let myself be discouraged by the bad. I'll try to focus only on what's good. Okay. I see kids with guns on TV—and once you see them, it's too late, isn't it? They're mug shots! But then I walk past our playground where laughter splashes down slides, and joy spins around on the merry-go-rounds, and I feel reassured again that God is still in control. Why did I doubt it?"

"Well, I don't blame you." Marge swiped a lick of batter. They stood for a moment, each absorbed in her own thoughts, until Marge turned to run water for the dishes. "I vote for Cordelia's theory on the theft. It definitely has to be that sneaky Avery bunch. We used to call them 'river rats' back in high school!"

She sighed.

"Yeah, rats are sneaky," Gracie agreed, knowing her friend was teasing.

"Seriously, though, I don't think that pitcher and bowl were taken for the money. After all, quite a few of those items were more valuable. Howie Anderson's rifle, for one. Then there's Dr. Ebersole's mother's silver tea service. Cordelia said it's pre-Revolutionary.

"No, that pitcher and bowl must have sentimental value to someone, I just know it. It can't have just been that they were the easiest to snatch." Marge furrowed her brow.

"I've been thinking the same thing," Gracie admitted. "Rocky, though, feels sure that the culprit is Carl Jackson—even though he has an alibi. But Herb is equally positive that it can't be Jackson, claiming his alibi is airtight."

"Gosh, we're beginning to sound like TV detectives," Marge said. "Motives and alibis—what next? A trenchcoat?"

Gracie still looked serious.

"So, let's hear your theory. Who might have some reason to feel a connection to the pitcher and bowl?" Marge leaned against the counter to listen.

"Deborah Jackson, for one. It was in the house she inherited from her aunt. As far as I've been able to determine, her great-aunt Agatha lived there most of her life. Before that, it belonged to a man named Jasper Marshall."

"So, what are you going to do about her?"

"Rocky actually believes Deborah might open up to someone she considers a friend—and she did offer to show me her orchids."

"Hey, I love orchids, too!"

Deborah's greenhouse was small but beautifully tended.

"My orchids love Bach," she told them. "And I play Handel's *Messiah* during Advent. You should see the Christmas cacti! They practically purr!"

Marge looked at Gracie, who smiled. Somehow they both understood intuitively that Deborah Jackson had not stolen the pitcher and bowl.

Gracie decided to pray for Deborah as they walked through the massed orchid plants, the air damp with mist and sweet with orchid nectar. She felt certain that this was the place her new friend met the Lord, much the same way Gracie did in her kitchen.

These flowers are Your bounty and Your grace. Let her continue to know peace here and to draw strength from Your wondrous creation.

"Carl works all the time," Deborah told them, leading them out of the greenhouse into her flower beds. She paused, obviously proud of her colorful perennials, brilliant in the sunlight, their leaves seeming almost polished green. "Since the children left, this has become my life. My youngest is twenty-five and lives in Chicago. My next lives back East. My older daughter is in San Diego. Her husband's in the Navy, an officer on a submarine."

"Do you have grandchildren?" Gracie wanted to know.

Deborah shook her head. "Holly has only been married a year."

Gracie then mentioned her own family, and Deborah

seemed to mean it when she asked if she had any pictures. Why was no one surprised that she just happened to have a wallet-sized family portrait of Arlen and his wife, Wendy, and of course, her darling grandson, Elmo, the spitting image of his grandpa? "El would be so proud," she told Deborah. "He was so excited whenever he envisioned those grandchildren who would be appearing in our life."

"I wish Carl felt the same." Deborah sighed, and changed the subject. "I'd always dreamed of having a garden like this. Aunt Aggie's generosity has provided it. It gives me pleasure, now that my son and daughters are grown and gone. I do miss them."

"Your borders really are impressive," Marge complimented her.

"So, you garden and your husband collects antiques. The right teamwork to benefit such a lovely old house!" Gracie wondered if she was being too effusive.

"Carl sells antiques, but he doesn't have time for a hobby as such," Deborah explained. "I told you, I inherited all this. Carl's interested in books and in clocks, but his work is his main thing. Everything else comes after it."

Gracie looked at her expectantly.

"Even me." Deborah gave a short laugh.

Marge and Gracie looked at each other.

"Would you like a cup of tea?" Deborah now inquired. Gracie noted that she was rubbing the space on her ring finger.

Over Earl Grey and scones, she spoke of their former home on Long Island, where Carl had worked as an art dealer. Their life in Willow Bend she described, however, as a new beginning.

"But starting again so far from what you know well is hard. I do miss the friends I had," Deborah told them. "And, I told you, Carl's almost never home. If he isn't in Chicago wheeling and dealing collectibles, he's in his office, or on the Internet, trying to find more to sell."

A man in that business certainly should have known the exact value of that pitcher and bowl, Gracie thought to herself.

"Is that where he finds the clocks?" Marge wanted to know.

Gracie glanced around the breakfast nook. A dome clock graced the buffet, and a Swiss pendulum marked the hour with a pair of ice skaters. The ticking would take a little getting used to, Gracie decided.

Deborah nodded. She rubbed her finger again.

"But the pitcher and bowl came with the house, right?" Gracie confirmed. "I think your husband told the police the set was a family heirloom."

"Aunt Agatha had long rented out the second-story apartment in the carriage house but furnished it with pieces— odds and ends—from the house. When we got here, I recognized many of them from my childhood visits. Lots were unfamiliar, though.

"She always thought of herself as a trustee, incredibly blessed to have inherited this mansion. When she was younger, she would willingly accommodate missionaries on home leave and other sojourners in need of a place to stay for an extended period. They were her primary tenants. In both of these buildings, she was perfectly at ease using valuable heirlooms in her everyday life. And it gave her pleasure to share them with these guests."

Gracie had known Deborah's relative slightly but never realized that her spirit was so large.

"Carl wanted something a bit more modern, so now the second floor is a combination office and studio apartment."

Gracie pressed on, "I'm curious. I know a little of the history of this place, but probably not all."

"My aunt was a nurse. Jasper Marshall was a paraplegic. His back had been broken in an accident when he was a young man. Neither Jasper nor Aggie ever married. My great-aunt was quite young when she came to work for him. He was much older and became like a father to her, so it made sense he would leave her the house."

Deborah's face paled, and Gracie felt a chill. Turning to look in the direction of the woman's stare, she saw Carl in the doorway. How long had he been standing there?

Deborah quickly explained that Gracie and Marge had come to see her orchids. His greeting seemed cordial, and so Gracie tried not to judge him. But, as he reminded Deborah of something he'd asked her to do that she'd forgotten, she couldn't help sense the disdain he felt for his wife.

Gracie and Marge excused themselves.

"He's a control freak," Marge said, sliding into the passenger seat. "The clocks gave him away before I ever met him. Imagine living with that tick-tick-tick day in and day out. It's like water torture but, unfortunately, it's one she's gotten used to!"

ROCKY WAS DEEP in conversation with Uncle Miltie when Gracie got home. He'd dropped in, sniffed out the lasagna and had patiently waited to tell her that it came close enough to his Italian standard that he'd consent to eat it.

"Staying to dinner?" Uncle Miltie chuckled. "You know that means you have to laugh at my jokes!"

Rocky rolled his eyes. "What do you think I've been doing for the past hour?"

They'd barely said grace when her uncle launched his first assault. Gracie and Rocky chewed in silence.

"The passengers on a plane were waiting for the flight to leave. Then the entry door opens and two men walk up the aisle dressed in pilot uniforms. Both are wearing sunglasses.

One is led by a seeing-eye dog, while the other taps his way up the aisle with a cane. Nervous laughter spreads through the cabin, but the men enter the cockpit, the door closes, and the engines start. The plane moves faster and faster down the runway, and passengers realize that they're headed straight for the water. Everybody starts screaming, and at that moment the plane lifts smoothly into the air."

Uncle Miltie grinned, apparently savoring the punch line.

"'Up in the cockpit, the co-pilot turns to the pilot and says, 'You know, Ed, one of these days, they're going to scream too late, and we're all gonna die.'"

Rocky groaned, as was expected.

Gracie dished out the salad.

"I love Caesar salad," Rocky exclaimed. "Are there a few more of those homemade croutons?"

"El always loved them, too."

Now, as he took a second serving of lasagna, it was Rocky's turn to offer an update. He'd checked up on the appraiser, who'd turned out to have a slightly shady original reputation. Still, the man was legitimate and, when questioned about the Jacksons' claim that the bowl had a unique mark that made it more valuable, he'd been frank. He'd admitted that he'd simply been giving an evaluation for an insurance policy, not for a scholarly review. Something perfunctory had been all that was required of him.

"What did you expect?" Uncle Miltie asked rhetorically.

Gracie then told them about encountering Carl earlier in the day. "We decided he was a real control freak. You know, a perfectionist and a drill sergeant all rolled into one."

Rocky listened intently.

"But what bothers me," Gracie went on, "is that I just can't believe he wasn't aware from the start of the value of that pitcher and bowl. This guy deals in antiques and collectibles."

"But we can't prove anything," Rocky reminded her.

"Earlier, before I met him, I was so sure he didn't do it. Now I don't know. Rocky, what happens if he wins the suit? Does the church have to pay?"

"He's going after the town. His lawyer merely included the church as back-up."

Gracie still looked worried.

"Well," cracked Uncle Miltie, hoping to divert her, "speaking as one antique whose value is beyond the powers of all appraisers save one"—he glanced heavenward—"I'm ready for dessert. How about you two?"

Gracie always enjoyed the break between Sunday school and worship. It gave her a chance to relax, change gears, and to visit with those folks who had attended the earlier service.

"Hi, Mrs. Parks!" Corey Bower flashed silver-studded teeth sporting neon-orange rubber bands. "What's up?"

"The ceiling?"

He giggled, and so did she.

"How are you?" Gracie loved chatting with the kids. "Your mom says you took first place in the county swimming league. That's great!"

He shrugged. "I won a trophy—that was my goal. This year, I'm at the top of my age group, but next season I'll be swimming against older kids, so I figured it was now or never."

"Gotta go," Corey announced. "See you, Mrs. Parks!" And then, "Bye, Mom!" to his mother who'd just walked up to them.

He waved and dashed out the door.

Marybeth shook her head. "To have that much energy!"

Gracie waved Marge over to join them as they prepared to join the choir in the robing area.

Marybeth, reporting on the progress of the quilt and banner projects, told them there was good news. "We've had a lot of response to the request we put in the bulletin. And Comfort has cut and provided muslin rectangles so there can be some continuity."

"I took one for each of us," Gracie told her, "but I really don't know what to do with mine. I'm not very artistic. Uncle Miltie has an insignia he got from one of his veterans' reunions. He wants me to sew that on his banner. I was kind of hoping we would do something together."

"Use a coloring book and trace something," Marybeth suggested. "You can embroider it, or use those fabric paints.

And since Gooseberry can't make his own, you, of course, have to include a cat."

Marge had an idea: "A cat and a casserole! Like a coat of arms!"

"Bet you hadn't thought of that," Marybeth said. "I sure hope a lot of people accept the challenge. The more families participate, the more thrilling it will be. I get goosebumps just thinking of them all—so many special glimpses into the lives of our friends and neighbors!"

Comfort joined them. Next to her, clutching her hand, was Lillian whose grin revealed a missing bottom tooth.

"Look at you!" Gracie said, crouching to admire the gap.

"Tooff Fairy gave me a silver dollar."

Marge pretended to wiggle a tooth in her own mouth. "A silver dollar! I thought she only gave a nickel a tooth! Think I can get one of these out?"

Lillian protested. "You're too big."

Marge shed a mock tear, wiped it away and they all laughed. Lillian, extremely pleased with herself, headed off to join some other squealing children who looked to be having more fun than the grown-ups.

"I'm taking my family quilt to Cordelia after church," Marybeth told them. "Her plan has always been for it to be in the library exhibit. I got my calligraphy kit and sat down and wrote up a history of it. I was going to drop it off before this, but I knew I needed to keep it by me for inspiration."

She looked at Comfort. "Would you like to come along?"

"I-I'm not sure what we're doing this afternoon. We usually like to do something as a family on Sunday afternoons. Thanks for the invitation anyway."

Gracie was sure Comfort hadn't said anything to Marybeth about the quilt. She was also sure the suspicions about its true origins would have to be voiced eventually.

"I'm so excited. I wrote some of its history on nice parchment—even burned the edges to make it look like it had lasted through fires and famine! You know, a genuine antique document!" Marybeth's dimples made her look girlish. "Just don't show it to any experts! I loved the calligraphy course I took before the kids came along, but since I've been home-schooling them, things like that are pure luxury. This was an excuse to indulge myself—plus it honors my great-great-aunt." She smiled as Lillian ran up to her mother.

"She's a cutie. And she has your total attention. Twins make that impossible."

"Any leads on the theft?" Comfort wanted to know.

"Herb's got a pesky insurance investigator to deal with, so he's been a bear these last couple of days. I don't dare ask him anything, for fear he'll tell me!" Marybeth laughed.

Gracie secretly held out hope that Arlen and Wendy would one day choose Willow Bend over New York as a place to raise her grandson. What a joy it would be to see them become friends with couples like the Bowers and Hardings!

Gracie's thoughts returned to Comfort's genealogical research. "Did you get a chance yet to talk to Dr. Dave?" Gracie asked Comfort. "What did you learn?"

They all knew the veterinarian Davena Wilkins. She had grown up in Willow Bend, but then she and her parents had moved out West. Only as an adult and a qualified doctor had she returned. Her history was one piece of the patchwork story of Willow Bend's African Americans, and that was what interested Comfort.

"She's going to write her mom and dad. They're in Arizona. But whom I really want to talk to is Charlie Harris. He's the one with the interesting history."

"It's sometimes hard for me to figure out what he's talking about," Marybeth said. Like most Willow Benders, she took Charlie for granted and thought of him as backward, if she thought of him at all.

"I've found him to be quite shrewd," Marge said, glancing at Gracie. "In his own way. He always knows what's going on. He may not have a college degree, but he makes a living and takes care of himself."

"I'm sorry," Marybeth said, her tone reflecting her embarrassment. "I just meant that he might be hard to interview."

Comfort shrugged. "I won't know until I try."

Gracie dropped by to see Phyllis Nickolson later that day,

hoping to find out a little more about Deborah Jackson. Phyllis, the switchboard operator at Keefer Memorial, was a clearinghouse for information about her fellow citizens, she always found. It was a beautiful evening and, after rocking the Nickolsons' new baby to sleep, Gracie joined her friend on the front porch.

"That was a treat!" Gracie sat down beside her on the swing. "I didn't get to rock Elmo nearly enough."

"Who is Elmo?" Katie, Phyllis's daughter by her first marriage, sat on the steps playing and reading a book.

"He's my grandson," Gracie told her. "He lives with his parents in New York."

She nodded. "Does he go shopping at Macy's? I love the Christmas movie with that Santa Claus who's so cool! I always wanted to go to Macy's. Has he ever seen the parade? Did he ever go to the Statue of Liberty?"

"He just turned five!" Gracie laughed. "We've seen the Statue of Liberty, but I don't think he's too interested in shopping yet."

"I'm going to go to New York City someday. Maybe I'll be a model or a Broadway star." She rolled her eyes. "Willow Bend is *sooo* boring!"

"Don't you have to write a report for school tomorrow?" her mother wanted to know.

"Your *husband* is on the computer," the girl said with disdain.

Gracie had hoped things had gotten easier for Phyllis. Katie had been quite jealous of Darren Michael when they first brought him home from the hospital. Although second marriages and blended families were the reality for many children, Gracie understood they were not easy to navigate. Phyllis and Terry were obviously trying hard. *They just need a little help from You, Lord.*

Gracie smiled at Katie. "Your stepdad is pretty proud of you. He told me about the art award you won."

Katie shrugged. "He's okay." And to her mother. "Better than okay, I guess."

"I bet if you tell him you have a paper due, he'll give you the computer. Probably even help you."

Katie brightened quickly and, forgetting her pique, went inside.

"It's tough parenting a 'tween." Phyllis sighed.

Gracie patted her friend. "We'll keep praying. She might rebel, but our prayers are her anchor. God gave her to you knowing everything you were going to go through, so He's right there with all of you. She won't stray far. He's got her safe and snug." Phyllis looked grateful.

As they chatted about the hospital, Gracie seized the opening she'd been looking for. "Deborah Jackson invited me over to see her greenhouse. I'm just getting to know her, but she seems nice. Do you know her very well?"

"I haven't talked to her much lately," Phyllis said. "We

used to eat at the same time. But these days she takes the graveyard shift so the nurses with young children can be at home. I don't even bump into her. I do hear how she's become a skilled hand with the lunar loonies, though."

Gracie was perplexed.

"I mean those strange folks who tend to show up when the moon's full." Phyllis laughed. "You wouldn't believe some of them! Deborah's always calm and known for her no-nonsense nature. She's so indispensable when it comes to these off-the-wall cases that some of them even ask for her on their repeat visits."

Phyllis confirmed what Gracie had already determined: Deborah Jackson was a good woman. How could she possibly be the culprit?

"*Mmm*, just look at that sunset," Phyllis said, pointing to the rose-and-magenta-streaked sky in front of them.

Gracie recalled a particular sunset years earlier, when she and El were still young parents. They'd just tucked Arlen in and sat on a swing like this one while their baby son slept soundly beside them in his bassinet. She could almost feel El slip his arm around her. It made her shiver, but the sensation was a pleasant one.

"A penny for your thoughts?" It was Phyllis asking, but Gracie heard her husband's voice.

She closed her eyes. "Beginnings and endings seem to blur in sunrise and sunset."

At that moment, she felt so close to God. She had just tucked a baby in for the night, and now she was remembering how she'd once worried about what kind of parent she would be. Next to her sat another young mother, also concerned about whether or not she was doing a good job. It was a lovely continuum.

The Lord had once met Gracie on an evening a lot like this one, helping her to face the same doubts. Thinking it over, Gracie understood that children slept soundly, despite their parents' worries. They rested in God's love, and it would always be so.

She smiled at the young mother beside her. "The sky is earth's security blanket," she told Phyllis happily. "And God has perfect taste in color."

G RACIE STOPPED AT THE CHURCH on her way home from the library. Barb was finalizing the order for the new robes that afternoon, so choir members were coming and going to the vesting room. Gracie called out a hello to Roy Bell, who was talking to Don Delano in the parking lot. Roy was the church troubleshooter, taking his job as head of the Property Committee very seriously.

When it was Gracie's turn to check in with Barb, Estelle was still there, throwing a small fit. Her insistence that a "medium" robe was the correct size for her had caused Barb to balk. And there apparently was no compromise position.

Gracie confirmed her own size, the same one she'd been wearing for years. Barb was now silently counting to ten while Estelle glowered at her. Gracie wasn't sure if any interference from her would help or hinder.

"What we need is a tailor," Estelle announced. "Since we're spending all this money for new robes, they should fit right! It embarrasses me to see us look so dowdy beside Waxman Tabernacle. I am sure our anonymous benefactor wants the best for us!"

She grew more excited. "And, speaking of professional—why didn't we hire a reputable company to trim those limbs in the churchyard? That Charlie Harris is going to make a mess of things, mark my words." This last was punctuated with a little snort.

"We don't know that, Estelle." Barb glanced at Gracie for support. "Cordelia's landscaping is lovely, as you well know, and Charlie does almost all of her work. What's more, I've seen him at the Jackson mansion."

"He works for Deborah?" Gracie's perked up her ears at this news.

Barb shrugged. "I've seen him trimming shrubbery."

"Well, bushes are hardly trees. I'm just praying he doesn't kill a tree or chop his own arm off for that matter."

Gracie knew that Estelle had a softer side. If she could only figure out how to keep it in the forefront—but on days like this, finding it at all seemed a daunting task.

"Well, prayer is just the insurance we need." She smiled at Estelle. "After all, everything goes better with prayer!"

And with that, Gracie excused herself, heading to the office to make some copies of discussion questions for her next Sunday school class. She was hoping to have a word with Pastor Paul, as well. Possibly he had come to some new conclusions about the troubling theft.

"Hi, Gracie!" Pat Allen sat at her computer with her back to the door, an aria playing softly in the background.

"How did you know it was me?"

The church secretary spun her chair to face forward. "You've been wearing that same perfume as long as I can remember." Gracie remembered how much her son as a small boy had liked it. She hadn't always worn the expensive scent, but had loved to sample it whenever she and Arlen passed the counter at the Mason City department store. Wishing she could afford some, she told her young son as much. Later, Arlen had led his dad to that atomizer, insisting he buy his mommy some. They had been treating her to it ever since, Arlen continuing the tradition after his father died.

In a blink, grief washed over her once again, its sad sweetness attesting to the value of life.

Thank You, Lord, for memories.

Pat was staring at her. "You okay?"

"El bought me my first bottle of this perfume."

"It's lovely. He had good taste." Pat didn't speak for a long moment, but her silence said enough. She understood that Gracie needed the space to remember.

Gracie handed Pat the questions to copy and asked if Paul was around.

"He has a ministerium meeting this morning," Pat said, positioning the original on the glass plate of the copier. "And it's his turn to lead the weekly Bible Hour at Pleasant Haven. Given everything, I don't expect him back until late this afternoon."

She faced Gracie, as the machine produced the dozen copies asked for. "So what do think about these thefts? I know our police chief is only doing his job, asking me so many questions—but it was unnerving being grilled like I was a common criminal. And by a friend, no less!"

"I know Herb hates being in this position. I hope your answers were at least of some help."

"No, I think I only frustrated him more. Nobody came by the office that morning. And I missed the Founders Day preview, so he didn't get much information from me." She smiled. "Paul said you had a great turnout that afternoon. I was glad to hear that, anyway."

"If the kick-off reception hadn't been such a success, this case might be easier to solve. Too many people altogether! I don't envy Herb. He has quite a list of folks to question."

"Well, I'm still sorry I missed the preview. Paul said you did your usual great job with the catering." Pat handed Gracie her copies. "Emily and I are trying to get Mother situated at Pleasant Haven. Now that our father's gone, she just rattles around that big old place. She wants to move, but there are a lot of memories to deal with."

Pat looked sad now herself. "I never thought I'd see the day when we would switch roles, my mother and I. She's always been so independent. Up until Daddy's death, that is." Again Pat's expression was regretful. "That took a lot out of her, I'm sure you understand."

Gracie put her hand on Pat's shoulder. "How about I stop by and see her? It is tough to be on your own after you've been sharing someone else's life for almost a half century. Her best times involved your dad, so she can't enjoy her own memories without thinking of him. Anywhere she goes, she's reminded of the life they shared. Even looking into your blue eyes, Pat, she sees your father."

Pat nodded. "I know. That's why we thought moving to Pleasant Haven would be good for her. A nice little efficiency apartment—a fresh start! She can eat in the dining room if she wants, or cook her own meals. Emily and I can visit her easily. It's just tough, Gracie. I'm making decisions I never thought I would have to make."

"She'll be okay." Gracie was sure of it, and offered up a prayer for Pat, her mother and sister. Gracie understood all too well the breadth of mourning and depth of grief yet unfinished.

"Thanks."

"She'll be okay," Gracie promised.

Pat smiled. "We always convince ourselves that it will be better tomorrow after we've accomplished the latest challenge.

But each tomorrow always hold its own challenges, right, Gracie?"

She nodded.

"Funny, I used to think things would be better once I conquered the obstacles in my life, but then I realized that obstacles *were* my life. Might as well lean into them, right? Now I try to give them all the muscle I have and count on faith to supply my joy."

Gracie simply listened.

"Mom needs me right now. And getting her settled is just the latest obstacle. I sure could use the prayer support."

Pat walked her to the outside door. "That Charlie Harris is a good worker, I don't care what anyone says. He's been here early the last few days, even before me." She pointed to where he was trimming trees. "We'd pay an arm and a leg to have a professional do that job. But Charlie says, 'a good wage for a good day's work, that's enough.'"

She looked at Gracie. "There's a lesson in that for all of us."

Amen, Gracie thought.

Pat continued. "He got the worst of the branches out the other day. It always makes me laugh, him on that crazy vehicle of his. Even if he relies on pedal power to get him around town, he still needed a chain saw."

Pat grinned. "At first, I thought 'no way!' But boy, he could sure wield that thing!"

They watched the odd but likable handyman haul the big limbs to his bicycle-driven cart.

Charlie was an enigma. People judged him thick witted, foolish or just plain eccentric, but no one really knew the man. He'd fabricated his own quite reliable vehicle, however zany it looked, and that took more ingenuity than most folks imagined. But, most of all, he was always dignified, even behind the wheel of his machine.

She walked over to talk to him. "You've done a nice job," she told him, scanning the area. "Looks like you've pruned every tree in the park."

"Job worth doing is a job worth doing right."

He doffed his battered felt hat. "Meemaw always told me that." Charlie's transparent fondness for his grandmother softened his features and endeared him all the more to Gracie.

"She must have been a wise woman."

He grinned. "She raised me good. Didn't have parents."

"I'm sorry."

"No need. I didn't know my mama and papa. I was too little. They was killed when our house burned. Terrible fire, spreading flames to our barn and carriage house. I don't remember much before I knew Meemaw's singing. I heard that good.

"We was the only ones not killed. Meemaw wrapped her

and me in a wet blanket. We slept in the same room, we did. 'Protect us Jesus!' she sang. I can remember that. She was a-rocking-and-a-singing. She just sang away what was bad then.

"I felt safe."

He looked at Gracie with a clear gaze. "I didn't know my mama and papa was gone 'til the next day. Meemaw said she sang me into the bosom of Abraham that night, and he held me tight so I could sleep, not knowing the sadness we faced. I believe that to be the truth."

Gracie nodded, not knowing what else to say.

"Sweet Jesus protected us that night, all right," Charlie told her. "Mr. Jasper was there. He done appeared out of nowhere. He led us out of the burning house. Meemaw said he was the angel of the Lord with flesh and bones."

Gracie remained quiet.

"Sweet Jesus saved our lives, yes ma'am," Charlie paused, seeming to reflect on that reality. "Sweet Jesus waked Mr. Jasper out of a sound sleep. And Mr. Jasper, he don't wake up less someone does some fierce shaking. The Lord shaked Mr. Jasper. He got out of his bed and followed the smoke.

"His brother Mr. Harmon was already there, but didn't know what to do. Then he heard my Meemaw singing. We was in the back of the house, on the first floor. My mama and papa was upstairs asleep. . . ."

He paused for long minute. "Missus Parks, nobody does

nothing that the Lord don't already know. The Lord God Almighty, He knows everything. He even knows how many hairs is on our heads."

Charlie laughed, rubbing his own. "Mine is easy to count these days. But there was time I had more. I don't remember losing all of them, but I did. It's not like misplacing something—when they're gone, they're gone."

Gracie was even more impressed with this man. God had a knack of revealing the profound in the simple. "You are so right, Charlie, God does know everything. Thank you for reminding me of that."

"Why, Missus Parks! Thank Him, not me." He scratched his head underneath his hat.

"I got to be getting back to work." Charlie paused and smiled. "I was here the other night, came back to get the clippers I left hanging in the tree. The windows was open, and you all were singing so pretty."

So the choir practice had had an audience!

"You was singing songs my Meemaw taught me. I told Missus Harding those songs was in my heart. I liked your choir singing those songs, Missus Parks. Just wanted you to know that."

She smiled. "Thank you, Charlie."

"Work's waiting."

She helped Charlie with the small branches he had yet to gather, coaxing him to tell her more about his grandmother.

She discovered that Cordelia's family had taken them in after the cabin burned, and that he lived there until his grandmother's death in 1954. Then he bounced around as an itinerant farmhand, living in bunkhouses and barns until Cordelia's father died. He was her only boarder until she opened her house up to the public in 1976.

"Mizz Cordelia is a fine lady," Charlie told her. "She needs me to look after her. So, I stay on, do them chores that need doing. Help her as I can."

Gracie smiled. "I know she appreciates you."

They had thrown the last of the brush on Charlie's cart when Marge walked across the parking lot to meet them. She had been to see Barb about her gown, requesting that her new one be just a bit longer in length.

Charlie tipped his hat. "Got to be going. Hammie Miller needs me." Pedaling off, he dodged a parked car to reach the street just as a pickup rounded the corner.

She heard a screech of brakes!

Gracie went running, Marge behind her.

Thankfully, Roy Bell had stopped just short of hitting Charlie.

"Charlie Harris!" Roy threw open the door of his pickup and hopped out. "That was a near miss! What if I hadn't been able to stop in time?"

Charlie just sat there in his home-built truck. Gracie wondered if he might be in shock, and hurried to his side.

She touched his shoulder. "Are you okay? Let me help you out!"

"Is he all right?" Marge wanted to know, taking Charlie's other arm. He was trembling. "Do you think he's in shock?"

"Have you got your cell phone on you?" Gracie asked Marge, who nodded. "Call for help then, please."

"I, I didn't see him!" Charlie looked like he would cry. "I didn't see the truck!"

Gracie rubbed his back. "It's all right, no one was hurt. Roy's just glad you're in one piece."

"I want to go home!"

"I'll take you, but I think we ought to stop at the hospital," said Gracie.

His gaze was imploring. "I just want to go home. No hospital!"

"Do you think he's okay?" Roy asked Gracie.

Charlie kept repeating that he wanted to go home, over and over. There was a stubborn set to his shoulders.

Roy crouched down to talk to him. "I was the one not paying attention. I should have seen you, really, Charlie, it's not your fault." He reached out to touch the man. "Come on, I'll see you get home. I've got a trailer hitch," he told Gracie. "I'll tow his vehicle back to Cordelia's, or just put it in the bed of the pickup if it will fit."

"Roy wants to help. We'll work this out. It's going to be okay, Charlie." She spoke softly to the distraught man.

"I want to go home," he said simply. "Home."

Marge appeared with her cell phone to her ear. "I took a chance and asked for Deborah to be paged," she said, covering the mouthpiece. "I figured she could advise us as to whether or not we should take him to the emergency room."

She removed her hand. "*Umm-hmm.* Yeah, he's sitting here with Gracie. He looks okay, but I can't tell. Okay." She handed the phone to Gracie.

"Marge says Charlie seems confused," said Deborah on the other end. She was all business. "Try to get him to look at you. Study his pupils. Are they dilated? Is he coherent? Can you tell?"

Gracie now coaxed Charlie to sit up, and questioned him about what had just transpired. "He could have had a seizure. We have no way of knowing why he pulled out in front of the other driver. And I'm concerned he may be in shock," Deborah was saying to her.

Gracie studied the man. "He wants to go home" is all she could think of in reply.

"He should be seen by a physician. I think you need to bring him here."

For Charlie, that might very well make matters worse. "He really just wants to go home. He seems all right."

"Gracie, just for everyone's peace of mind, please bring him to the hospital." Deborah paused. "He's worked for me, and I do care that he's seen to properly. Don't take the responsibility for something that may backfire on you. Bring him here to the emergency room. He knows me, and I'll be waiting for you."

Charlie looked at Gracie. "Home," he repeated.

"I know, Charlie. We just want to make sure that you are really okay."

"Let me talk to him," Deborah now requested. Gracie complied and soon noticed that Charlie was calmer. Whatever Deborah was saying seemed to be putting him at ease.

"Let me call Cordelia," Roy suggested. "I've got a cell phone in my pickup. The doctor may want to talk to her. He might require her to sign medical forms."

Gracie lowered her voice, stepping out of Charlie's earshot. "He's an adult, and I don't imagine she has any more legal connection to him than I do, even if he boards with her."

"He might be an adult, Gracie, but you're wrong about one thing: Cordelia is his guardian. Her daddy and his grandmother took care of that. Plus, she and Charlie actually own that tourist home together."

Those pieces of information came as a shock. "Are you really serious? Cordelia is Charlie's guardian? They own her house together?"

"I found out during the renovation work I did when she decided to take in paying guests."

"Anyway," Roy finished up, "all that paperwork hit Cordelia hard. Too much red tape. Too many permits to secure. What I did was help her out with it all, and so I learned a lot about her finances and the way her deed was set up."

"The truth is, Charlie's money is providing for them both. You don't think she makes a living with the few tourists who stay there, now do you?"

Appearances certainly were deceiving. Cordelia played the grande dame, while to many people Charlie Harris was all but invisible.

At the hospital, Cordelia turned out to be waiting for them. She only relaxed once the doctor had assured everyone that Charlie checked out fine. "It's time to go home," she told him. "Mr. Bell brought your bicycle home, and I know you want to make sure it's okay." She slipped her arm through his. "I've got supper ready. Your favorite meatloaf."

"With green beans?"

"And mashed potatoes."

"Applesauce?"

"Of course."

Charlie grinned. "Sounds just right. I'm hungry."

Gracie couldn't help but agree with him. Back at her own house, sweet potato casserole and baked ham were on the menu. She would call Rocky and ask him to join them.

"Not too bad, Gracie my girl, not too bad at all," Uncle Miltie said, leaning back in his chair and patting his tummy. "By the way, I've been meaning to ask you two—do you have any notion which vegetable is the kindest?"

"Kind? Vegetables?" Rocky rolled his eyes. "Please."

"Sweet potatoes!" Only one person let out a guffaw.

Rocky shook his head. Uncle Miltie looked defiant.

"I've been working on your lead," Rocky now said to Gracie. "There's quite a lot of information about Jasper and Harmon Marshall in the county records and at the library. We were planning to run old photographs, ads and bits of news throughout the celebration, so the files have been getting quite a workout. But ours don't go back that far.

"Anyway, it seems their father ran something called Pittsburgh Outfitters. He also underwrote loans for folks heading to California on the Overland Trail."

Gracie began to clear the table for dessert. "So? What brought him to Willow Bend?"

"The railroad. He seems to have been a sharp businessman and smelled engine smoke in the winds of change. He was a major player in the merger of the Lake Shore and Michigan Southern Railway Companies. His obituary says that he was investigating routes when he stumbled on Willow Bend, loved the town and the location, and put down roots.

"Apparently, he built that place of Cordelia's to entertain railroad dignitaries and other guests. They actually lived in the Jackson place."

She opened the cupboard and reached for three mugs. "That doesn't connect him to our mystery."

"Nope, but I figure that's where you come in."

He sat back down and spooned sugar in his coffee. "What we have at the paper is bound in big books. No one's ever gotten around to microfilming them, so there isn't an index. It takes time and a keen eye." He smiled at Gracie. "I thought maybe you'd want to take a look. Your sleuth sense is pretty unbeatable. . . ."

Sleuth sense notwithstanding, this case had her baffled! "I've got some time tomorrow morning," she told him, but, inwardly, she felt as far from understanding what was going on as she ever had.

And she hadn't the slightest idea what she'd be looking for, once she began poring over old issues of the *Mason County Gazette*, either.

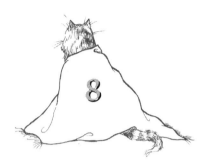

THE NEXT AFTERNOON while Gracie was washing the lunch dishes, Herb appeared at her back door. When she invited him in, he took off his hat and put it on the table before sitting down.

The police chief tried to be pleasant, making small talk, but Gracie could see that something serious had happened. "How's the mystery going? Any new leads?"

"Someone's taken Marybeth's family quilt."

Her jaw dropped.

"I haven't told her yet." He looked very unhappy. "It's going to knock her for a loop when she hears what happened to one of her prized possessions. Several loops, in fact."

"This is terrible."

"Isn't that the truth! The only good thing in this whole

case is the insurance investigator is as perplexed as I am."

Herb sighed. "He was suspicious of Carl Jackson because he'd just bought his policy."

Gracie watched him, feeling helpless.

"I asked the insurance guy if it wouldn't have been a whole lot easier if they'd checked the appraisal before issuing such a hefty policy. He says to them one of that size is small potatoes—until they have to pay it out, I guess."

"So Carl really is the most likely suspect?"

"Except that he was in Chicago—we've checked. He was at an antique auction, and they've verified it because he bought a few things. He paid with a credit card.

"But that doesn't exactly eliminate him. He could have put someone up to it."

"Like his wife?"

"I don't know. I hate to think Deborah was involved. I talked to her the morning the theft was discovered—she was certainly upset and not looking forward to what her husband was going to say."

He shook his head. "Marybeth is never going to understand. She thinks police work is like parenting—you question the suspect and they come clean, out of a guilty conscience. I hate to admit, but we just don't have a clue on this one."

He sighed. "I was hoping you'd go over and see Cordelia. She's pretty worked up about the whole affair."

Gracie had to admit she felt the same. "What about Marybeth?"

"I'm heading home next. I left Jim at the tourist home. We're going to try to get some fingerprints. Cordelia's a good housekeeper, and she says she thinks she's the only one who touched the table. But fingerprints won't find us a suspect."

"It could eliminate a few." Gracie was thinking of Deborah.

"Well, I've got to bite the bullet and go tell Marybeth." How unhappy he looked, Gracie thought.

She saw him to the door. "We're just going to trust that these things will be returned."

"You must have gone to the same school of investigation as my wife." It took an effort, but he chuckled. "She puts her faith in everyone's honesty."

"Maybe that detective work is kind of like driving in the dark. You can only see as far as the headlights. But you keep going, trusting your sense of direction. You'll get to the bottom of this, Herb. You always do."

"I hope you're right." He put a hand on her shoulder. "I really feel bad about this, Gracie. Marybeth loves that quilt. I don't how to tell her that it is gone. Say one of your prayers for me, will you? This is the toughest job I've had to do in a long time."

She promised she would.

When Herb left, Gracie called Marge and they headed over to the tourist home together. Cordelia was sweeping the already spotless front porch. "I've got to do something!"

The older woman gave the broom a hard swipe across the painted wooden floor. "I can't stop thinking about the quilt. I can't stop worrying about the reality that someone invaded my privacy. In all the years I've run this place, I've never had anything taken. Never even had reason to lock the doors leading to my private living space.

"Now, I suspect every stair creak and squeaking floorboard. I imagine intruders skulking about, searching for other valuables to steal."

She sat down on a padded rocker. "I suddenly feel old."

"Vulnerable," Gracie sympathized. "These thefts have us all unnerved. And Pastor Paul blames himself."

"The Historical Society certainly doesn't blame Paul Meyer," she assured them.

"Times are changing," Cordelia told them darkly. Marge and Gracie looked at each other, then made themselves comfortable in adjoining rocking chairs.

The rhythmic movement back and forth was comforting. It reminded Gracie of how she'd felt as she sat on Phyilis Nickolson's front porch and watched the sunset. "Don't lose heart," the old chairs seemed to plead.

Cordelia sighed. "I'm glad you stopped by," she admitted. They rocked companionably for several quiet moments. Wendell, Cordelia's fluffy black cat, padded by them, leaving a few meows trailing after him.

"What did you do today?" Gracie asked Cordelia. She said she had fixed a continental breakfast for her guests. They were a couple from Chicago on a leisurely trip to visit their children in Ohio. Besides Charlie, she had one other boarder, who had left for work early, as usual.

"Charlie left bright and early this morning to do that trimming at your church."

Marge had a thought. "We seem to have a choosy thief. He—or she—likes valuable Americana."

"That's a good point," Gracie conceded. "The antiques *were* displayed at the kick-off; in fact, part of the point was for the people to see them there. Plus, Marybeth had talked about her quilt there. She was excited about sharing it."

"But how would anyone know *I* had the quilt?" Cordelia asked.

Marge poured tea. "Marybeth had it at church and mentioned she was taking it to your house later on." She looked at Gracie. "But that implies the thief is a member of our congregation, and I'm having trouble with that."

"You're sure it couldn't have been one of the guests?" Gracie asked her.

Cordelia's "Absolutely!" was firm.

"Well, I guess this clears Carl Jackson of suspicion," Marge said. "But I still don't trust that guy. There's something about him that makes me go, 'Whoa!'"

"Well, Deborah's aunt was a fine woman," Cordelia told

them. "She was also a nurse. Agatha grew up in a foundling home, so she didn't have anyone. Neither did Uncle Jasper, for that matter."

"He was your uncle?"

"My father's brother. He was injured in a terrible fire that took a cabin, some outbuildings and the adjoining fields."

The older woman leaned back again, seeming to savor the warmth of her tea cup. "Two people in that blaze—a horrible tragedy.

Gracie and Marge were somber.

"Agatha answered an ad Uncle Jasper had put in the paper. She cared for him until he died. We all came to love her. They were very close, my uncle and Agatha, but there was nothing romantic between them.

She glanced at Gracie. "I was pleased when she inherited the house."

"Did you know Deborah?" Marge asked.

"She used to come here to visit when she was girl. She and her aunt seemed close, so it didn't surprise me when she left Deborah the house."

"It's baffling, that's all there is to it. Who has the motive to steal an antique pitcher and bowl and an heirloom quilt? That's what we have to figure out." Marge looked at Gracie.

Gracie couldn't help thinking there was a pivotal piece missing. Those heirlooms had something in common. She just didn't understand what it was.

Uncle Miltie and Rocky were sitting on the front porch when she returned from Cordelia's.

"Stopped by to update you on the case," Rocky said, standing to greet her. "The insurance company is going to pay Jackson's claim. The case is closed as far as they're concerned. Me, I still think the guy is guilty. So much for the objectivity of the press!"

He opened the door for her. "I can't write it, but I *can* think it."

Gracie sat on the chair across from him. "You heard about Marybeth's quilt?" He nodded, and she continued. "I need to tell you this. Just between us. Comfort Harding thinks it is really a slave quilt, created to guide runaways along the Underground Railroad."

Uncle Miltie whistled. "Never heard of that particular trick before. History still holds some surprises!"

Rocky looked thoughtful. "That gives the case an extra twist. Not that I know its significance, but it probably has some. These are both pre-Civil War artifacts."

"I've been thinking that there must be some common link between the two items," Gracie told him.

"Both are utilitarian in nature," Rocky added, "a bed cover and a pitcher and bowl for washing up."

Gracie couldn't help thinking that the only common link was Cordelia Fountain, but could that be true?

"All this detective work gives me a headache," Uncle Miltie said after a while. "We need a little diversion."

"A joke by some chance?" Rocky asked.

Uncle Miltie winked. "Beg me!"

"You wish!"

"An applicant was filling out a job application, see. And he came to the question 'Have you ever been arrested?' He wrote 'No.' The next question, meant for people who had answered 'yes' to the previous one, was 'Why?' The applicant answered it anyway: 'I never got caught.'" Uncle Miltie cocked an eyebrow.

Gracie pondered. "You think this is like our thief? That we'll know just how guilty he is only if we can catch him?"

"I'm still betting on Jackson," Rocky insisted. "The insurance policy, the lawsuit. That guy's just looking to cash in."

Gracie felt certain there was something they were not seeing.

But what was it?

Could Rocky be right—not about Carl Jackson, but in telling her she should trust her own sleuth sense?

G RACIE BOUNDED UP the choir loft steps, knowing after long experience just how to avoid the creaks. The last thing she needed was for Barb Jennings to stop playing! If only she could slip into her spot in the loft inconspicuously. She hated being late for anything, and especially choir practice!

"Choir practice starts and ends on time," Barb liked to say. In fact, she never seemed to stop trying to burn it into her choir's collective mind. Gracie herself normally liked to be on time—early, even. She'd always felt it was better to be three hours too early than even a minute late. El used to tease her about this very tendency of hers.

She paused to get her breath at the top of the steps.

Why hadn't I seen that gas gauge! I'm just too distracted, I guess, she thought to herself.

Thankfully, Fannie Mae had choked to a stop just blocks short of the Gas and Go. Harry Durant not only had provided a can for the gas, but also had given her a ride back to her car.

Thank goodness for good neighbors!

Gracie offered a grateful prayer for the owner of Willow Bend's most popular gas station and garage. Harry Durant was an opinionated man, it was true, but he was honest and an excellent mechanic. He also had made a difference in the life of Chuckie Moon and his buddies, by giving them jobs around the garage and space to work on their own cars. Which reminded her: She needed to check in with Pastor Paul to give him an update on her plans for Chuckie and company.

She had initially hoped the youth group could make Cordelia's basement a service project, but she now realized the space probably called for a smaller crew.

Gracie slipped in the door and quietly made her way to her seat. The air seemed charged, despite the soft strains of the praise chorus Barb was introducing. Gracie glanced around, trying to get a bead on what was going on.

Ah! One of their sopranos was absent. But Marybeth never missed choir practice! She looked forward to it, describing it as a better recharger of her batteries than any candy bar. And Gracie knew just what she meant.

She took her place next to Marge. The effect of having Marybeth's spot vacant created an uneasy sensation in her.

"Estelle said something to her," Marge whispered, handing Gracie her music folder. "Marybeth dashed out, crying, and Tish went after her."

Marge glanced toward Estelle, whose face was hidden by the music folder. "Her Highness over there said it was something Marybeth had a right to know, and that it wasn't any of our business."

Bert Benton leaned forward. "I knew Pastor Paul was in his office, so I called him on my cell phone. He met Tish and Marybeth in the vestibule. Tish came back and said Paul had taken Marybeth to his office. I gather that's where she is, still."

"Marybeth didn't tell Tish anything," Marge added.

Barb stopped playing and cleared her throat.

"Need I remind you that choirs and clocks are not mutually exclusive? We *will* finish punctually. We've got a lot to accomplish in a shorter period of time now."

"Too many queen bees in this hive," Marge said, under her breath.

Whew! Gracie's own tardiness turned out to be the least of anyone's concerns! She noticed Estelle watching her, so she smiled a greeting.

She didn't know what the conversation between Estelle and Marybeth had been about, but the woman was a sister in Christ. And sisters need to give each other the benefit of the doubt. Her voice pealed out, clear and true. "Lord, You know that, early or late, I'm singing my love for You."

After practice, Gracie apologized to Barb.

"Well," Barb said, stacking the music on the shelf, "I know you didn't mean to run out of gas. But that scene with Marybeth simply unnerved me! I just have no idea what happened! I know she's upset about her quilt, but when she came to practice she was in good spirits. Then, after the little chat with Estelle, she was in tears. What do you imagine our deadly diva said to her?"

Gracie ducked the question. "I think we have a wonderful choice of music for Founders' Sunday."

"Rick had suggested we include a couple of spirituals," Barb agreed. "I knew these two would be just right for our voices, and fitting, too, since all around here people were involved with the Underground Railroad. I just love 'Follow the Drinking Gourd.'"

"They're code songs?" Comfort had mentioned the Drinking Gourd being another name for the position in relation to Polaris or the North Star, and now Gracie saw the connections to the music, too. She described to Barb how Comfort was collecting local information.

"She's particularly interested in those African American families who have been in the area for generations."

"Well, one would be Charlie Harris," Barb told her. "His grandmother, Sadie Kindness, was born a slave, you know. I think Cordelia's great-grandfather bought her freedom. I remember Sadie coming to talk at school back in the fifties. I was barely a teenager, and she seemed old beyond my comprehension. No kid can imagine ever being a hundred years old, so she really stayed in my mind."

She had Gracie's attention. "Because she was so old?"

"No, because the story was so sad. Sadie's mother and father were childhood sweethearts, but her father wanted to be free. He kept trying to escape, until one day their master sold him to a man with a sugar plantation in the Caribbean. Sadie never saw her father again. But she and her brother escaped with their mother a short time later, by following a map her father had made."

"That's an amazing piece of local history."

Barb nodded. "It was written up in the newspaper, I know— but that was years ago."

Gracie made a note to mention that story to Rocky. Perhaps it could be found in the old files.

When she left Barb, she found Estelle waiting for her in the sanctuary. "Gracie, I'll walk you to your car."

"That would be nice." Gracie sensed the woman had something on her mind, and needed time to open up.

"I didn't mean to hurt Marybeth," Estelle began, tentatively. "I thought she should know the truth. I thought it would help. . . ."

She stopped and turned to Gracie, her gaze imploring. "I

overheard Comfort tell you about the quilt, and I thought telling Marybeth what I heard would make losing the heirloom easier to bear."

"Estelle!" Gracie exhaled frustration.

Lord, You're going to have to love her for me, because right now I want to throttle her!

"Do you think I ought to go see Marybeth and apologize?"

Gracie shook her head, not knowing how to respond. "You probably should see Comfort first. She shared her theory with me in confidence. She really didn't want Marybeth to know. You've hurt both of them, Estelle, but I'd start by making amends with Comfort first."

"I'm sorry, Gracie, I really am."

Pastor Paul was standing beside Fannie Mae, waiting for Gracie. He assured them that Marybeth was fine. "She's still convinced that the quilt was created by her ancestor." He looked thoughtfully at Estelle. "It's probably best for now if you hold off on repeating that story to anyone else."

"I won't say a word." Her tone was contrite.

It was getting late. Uncle Miltie was probably asleep in his favorite chair. Or Marge may have already roused him, and they were enjoying some leftover lemon pound cake with ice cream. Either way, Gracie needed to get home, so she excused herself.

"I talked to the insurance investigator today," Paul said, holding open her car door. "They're going to pay the claim.

But that doesn't mean the company's not concerned about how recently Carl Jackson had taken the policy out. I figured it was right around the time Mrs. Fountain approached them about lending the pitcher and bowl."

"But the investigator is satisfied?"

Paul shrugged. "There's nothing else he can do, especially taking into account the most recent theft."

"It's beginning to look like we're dealing with someone with very specific taste."

"So what's next on his list?"

That thought was unsettling!

Gracie was about to start Fannie Mae when her cell phone rang.

It was Cordelia calling from the hospital.

She told Gracie angrily that Chuckie Moon had pushed Charlie and that Charlie had fallen.

"A mild concussion?" Gracie repeated. "Oh, Cordelia, I'm so sorry!"

10

ITS NOT THE WAY IT SEEMS," Chuckie exclaimed, hurrying to meet Gracie at the entrance of the emergency room. "Nobody hurt Mr. Harris, honest, you've got to believe me!"

Quasi was beside him. "He tripped—I saw it!"

"Mrs. Fountain is in the examining room with the old guy now," Martin told her. "She told us to stay here until you arrived. She wanted to call the police, but then needed us to help her get Mr. Harris to the hospital. Good thing Chuck had his car! She was crying and acting so weird!"

Gracie put her hand on Chuckie's shoulder. "Start at the beginning. Exactly what happened?" The boy took a deep breath.

"How about we sit over there?" she suggested, pointing to the chairs in the waiting area.

Each of them seemed eager to tell the story from his own point of view. Gracie asked Chuckie to go first.

"We were cleaning out the debris in the entrance of the tunnel, just like Mrs. Fountain asked us, and Quasi was fooling around. He pushed me and I fell against the boards blocking the tunnel, and one splintered and gave way."

"I crawled through," Quasi interjected.

Martin added, "Because he's practically a midget."

Quasi shot him a smug look. "Sometimes small is good."

"Anyway," Chuckie went on, "I was looking for a flashlight so Quasi could see, when the old man comes at me. He's yelling and—"

"Waving an ax!" Martin said.

"Chuck didn't do anything to upset him," Quasi broke in. "I swear!"

Chuckie shook his head. "It wasn't actually an ax, just the handle. I think he was fixing it, because that's what I saw him doing when we got there. He has a grinder and a workbench in the basement."

"You know," Quasi said, "the whole time he kept watching us like we were going to rob the place or something."

Gracie looked at Chuckie. "He came at you with the ax handle?"

"Not exactly. He started yelling at us to stop fooling around. Quasi ignored him." Chuckie glared at his friend. "Then he told Quas to stay out of the tunnel, but he crawled through, anyway. So I was curious, too. He saw me get the flashlight. That's when he came after us with the ax handle. 'Mind your own beeswax!' he kept saying," Martin added. "Weird, huh?"

"I tried to crawl out," Quasi went on. "And Chuck was helping me. He gave me a yank, and he fell backwards and knocked the old man down. That's it. That's what happened."

Chuckie nodded. "We tried to tell Mrs. Fountain, but she was too upset. Mr. Harris kept saying we had to stop messing with the past, but he wasn't making sense."

"It was Chuckie who suggested we take him to the hospital," Martin told her. "He wasn't right, you could see it in his face. I know he's kind of slow and all, but that doesn't mean he's dumb. Plus, he's old. So we were worried when he started to get an expression on his face like some cartoon character seeing stars."

"Mrs. Fountain seemed fine until we got to the hospital. Then suddenly she got all mad again. She told me I was 'a bad apple' and a 'rotten egg' and that she going to call the police." Chuckie paused. "I pretty much begged her to call you first. I can't afford to get into more trouble, Mrs. Parks. I need scholarship money for college—I just can't manage without it!"

Quasi held his hands up in surrender. "That's the whole truth. And nothing but the truth. If anybody should get busted, it's me. I crawled through the stupid hole."

"I'll talk to Cordelia." Gracie closed her eyes for a moment, and quietly asked the Lord for guidance.

"Mrs. Parks?" It was Quasi.

"*Shh*, can't you see she's praying, stupid?" That was Chuckie.

Gracie reached to pat his leg. "Life is prayer, Chuckie. God is with us all the time. I was just listening. He gives me advice on how to handle difficult situations."

"So what did God say?" Martin seemed honestly interested.

"Be a friend, and trust Him."

"What do we have to lose?" Chuckie said. He grinned at Gracie. "Thanks."

When Cordelia and Charlie came out a little later with Dr. Hanley, he was cautioning Cordelia to keep an eye on the patient, too, for dizziness, irritability and memory loss.

"It was a mild concussion," Dr. Hanley told them. "But he'll be fine." And to the boys, he said, "He told us it was an accident. Mrs. Fountain is not going to press charges."

Charlie grinned. "You didn't mean no harm. I got scared, that's all. I feared the worst." He looked at Cordelia. "These boys didn't mean no harm. I know that."

"Okay, Charlie. I'll trust you." And to the boys: "Can you come back tomorrow after school?"

Their "Great!" was unanimous.

Gracie looked out her front window. It was a beautiful morning for prayer walking!

Gooseberry waited nearby, watching her.

"Not today, old boy. I'm visiting the Bowers, and I'm not too sure their German shepherd is fond of cats!" She stooped to pet him. "As much as you like to think you're a dog, my friend, a real canine may not agree. You just stay here and take care of Uncle Miltie."

She slipped on her backpack—inside it, a container of freshly baked brownies—and donned her headphones. After popping a favorite Southern gospel tape into her cassette player, she was ready to go. "See you later!"

Gooseberry jumped on the table in front of the window to watch her—or maybe the birds, she could never be sure which. Sunbathing and bird watching were her cat's favorite pastimes. She had to admit she liked both, as well.

Gracie set off on her daily four-mile trek. What had begun years ago as grief management had blossomed into an ongoing spiritual adventure. As she went on her way, Gracie often talked out loud to the Lord, sharing the joys and concerns of her heart.

Marybeth home schooled her twins, so the Bower kitchen was classroom, laboratory and pantry combined. This morning, Casey and Corey were concocting some kind of rubbery mixture they called 'slime'; but there was also a hint of maple syrup and vanilla in the air—pancakes for breakfast!

"Why don't we sit in the living room?" Marybeth said, as she watched the children recording the results of their experiment. "They've got assignments to complete." She eyed them, "And this mess to clean up. All good scientists keep a tidy laboratory!"

Gracie followed Marybeth into her comfortably cluttered family room. There the dog opened one eye briefly to check out the stranger.

"Marlin's a pussycat," Marybeth told her. But Marlin and Gracie were old friends and she gave him an ear-scratch in passing. He whimpered appreciatively.

Gracie felt the moment was now or never for talking to Marybeth about the quilt and Comfort Harding's theory.

"Really, Comfort had your best interests at heart. Although she herself feels fairly certain of the quilt's origin, she wasn't trying to make it a competition—her theory versus your knowledge of it."

Silence.

"Estelle is going to call you and apologize," Gracie said. "She knows she overstepped."

"She does like the power that having knowledge of secrets brings," Marybeth observed. "But she forgets how anyone else might feel."

"She promised Pastor Paul and me that she wouldn't say anything to anyone."

"But the quilt is gone." Marybeth's sadness was plain

to see. "So we'll never know which history was correct."

Gracie listened to her friend. Sad was better than angry.

"I do respect Comfort's opinion," Marybeth now said. "She seems to know a lot about quilts. But she *could* be wrong. I did a little checking of my own after Estelle's bombshell. On the Internet I found a site about the Underground Railroad, and it did mention the quilt codes.

"But, Gracie, it stated there is no real proof of their existence outside of oral tradition! The code simply made use of patterns common to quilts of the day, so how can we determine for sure which ones were used to guide runaways? They can't. That's why it remains in the realm of folklore. I can't blame Comfort for *wanting* it to be a slave quilt, because it would bring alive that important part of history, confirming it."

She met Gracie's gaze. "That quilt was made by my great-great-great-grandma, I am sure of it. She was nineteen years old and pregnant when she left Willow Bend to head west with her husband, and she was working on the quilt during the trip. I know those facts from the diary.

"The rest comes out of our own family history. She and her husband both died within a few years of each other in California. Their hired hand, a good friend from Indiana, brought their child all the way back to Velina's sister wrapped in the quilt."

Marybeth reached for the small leather book on the edge

of the table. "The journal mentions Velina working on a quilt for her baby. Our family history has its oral tradition, too, but at least we have this quilt and one journal. I always wanted to do some more research and see what I could learn about Velina, and I told Comfort that. She encouraged me, even though she believes my heirloom belongs to her own tradition."

Marybeth sighed. "It's so unexpected. Comfort and I were becoming good friends."

"And you still can be."

"I know you're right. I just need to stop feeling bruised."

Gracie pointed to the book. "May I?"

Marybeth nodded. "The entry about the quilt is marked."

Gracie opened the book to the page with a ribbon running down the center.

"August 15, 1861. We quilted until dusk. It's going to be a fine blanket. I sewed in pieces from Mama's party dress, and my Sunday frock. I hear the nights are cold in California and we'll need warm bedding."

"Is there more?"

"Isn't that enough? It came back with the quilt." Marybeth's calm was suddenly gone. "It was all we had of her memory. Now the quilt is gone, and everybody is questioning its authenticity!"

Gracie's heart went out to her.

"Gracie, who would steal my quilt? Who?"

Marybeth paused. "I don't want to be mad at Estelle—or Comfort, for that matter. I've just been praying that they find my quilt, and I don't even care whether or not we catch the thief."

They sat quietly for a couple of minutes, as Gracie browsed through the diary. Most of the entries were about the weather, trail and daily homemaking routine. "Imagine trying to bake a cake over a fire on a dusty trail," Gracie thought out loud. "And here Velina is cooking over a fire in the rain while another woman holds an umbrella!"

"These women were strong, and they loved their families. They did their best to make their wagons seem like a home."

"I'd like to know Velina better," Gracie told her. "Could I borrow her diary for a couple of days?"

Marybeth looked worried.

Gracie put the book on the table. "I'm sorry, how thoughtless of me. It's all you have left."

"No, really, Gracie, take it." She sat up and smiled. "I would be honored to have you read it.

"I'm ashamed of how I've been behaving. I've suspected just about everyone in the church. I know it's just a material possession, but it was so dear to my heart! I pray to let go of it and move on, but the sadness comes back and it's all I can think of. . . ."

"You have every reason to mourn the loss of something so special. God understands. You've been wise to go to Him in prayer. Keep it up, especially when you feel yourself getting upset. He'll help you through this time."

Gracie picked the little journal up and tucked it into her backpack. "I won't let it out of my sight."

"It's okay, Gracie, really. It's good for me to lend something again. And I trust you. Of course I do. Maybe there's a lesson for me in all this. I can be pretty possessive of things. Perhaps He let the quilt get taken so I would see that."

"God can use the worst of situations for good, you're right about that, but I don't think He would take your quilt to teach you a lesson. Your loss saddens Him, too. I'm sure of it. As I pray for all loved ones, including yourself, I realize they are in God's heart first. But not just my prayers are with you, so is my heart. And with Comfort, too."

Gracie slipped her arm around the woman. "I think the lost treasures are going to turn up, and if yours doesn't . . . well, you'll always have Velina's spirit around you. That's really the legacy, isn't it? We keep our loved ones alive in our memories."

"Oh, Gracie, the worst thing hasn't been losing the quilt. It's realizing how petty I can be. That's the tough lesson. I am not the Christian I want to be."

Gracie, too, had endured tough lessons in trying times. Perhaps that's what the Old Testament prophets meant about burning off the dross. Gold was purified by submitting it to intense heat; perhaps it was the same with character.

"We all fail, that's why we have the church. We can encourage each other. You fall down seven times, you get up eight. We ask for forgiveness and try again."

They went upstairs together. The kids had cleaned the kitchen, and were busy with text and notebooks at the table.

Marybeth paused at the door. "I'm glad you came. Herb says you and Rocky are helping him investigate. He appreciates your help, even if he doesn't tell you."

"We'll get to the bottom of this, Marybeth. I'm sure. I've got a feeling these heirlooms weren't taken for the money. I'm headed to the library this afternoon, to do some historical research."

"Historical research?" Marybeth chose her next words carefully. "Gracie, I've been wondering about a historical angle, as well. Cordelia Fountain *is* one common factor."

Gracie agreed, but she wasn't ready to speculate. "She's also one of Willow Bend's most respected citizens."

"I know." Marybeth averted her gaze. "But that isn't what I meant. It's Comfort I was thinking of. I can't help it. She does have a motive . . . and she knew Cordelia had the quilt."

"You really believe she'd steal your quilt?" Gracie strove to keep her tone gentle.

"She arrived at Cordelia's shortly after I did on Sunday. Remember her saying she couldn't go with me to deliver it because they did family things on Sunday? Well, I was just leaving when she appeared. And, if I'm not mistaken, I'd say by their conversation Cordelia had invited her."

"The quilt didn't turn up missing until midmorning the next day. You're not suggesting she broke into Cordelia's place as well, are you?"

"Her front door was open, Gracie. I walked right into Cordelia's living area. I knocked on the door dividing her private space, but it wasn't locked. I hate to say it, but it would have been easy to walk into that parlor and rob her blind. She would have never noticed."

Marybeth was plainly uncomfortable sharing her suspicion.

"I hate myself for this obsession about the quilt, but when Comfort's so interested in it and it disappears the day after she sees it, isn't it too much of a coincidence?"

Marybeth's jaw set. "As much as we hate to admit it, it *does* look like *someone* in our congregation is involved."

But Gracie was not satisfied. "There's a key piece missing to this puzzle. But for some reason—even if it's right in front of us—we're overlooking it."

"I hope you're right, Gracie. Like I said, I sense God is trying to teach me something in all of this. I want to trust Him . . . but I also want my quilt back. I can't help it."

She crossed her arms. "Herb feels the same way you do. I just want you all to cover all the angles, consider all the suspects. I don't want to think she did it, but I don't think we can rule her out, either."

Gracie prayed harder than she ever had for a glimpse of the truth. It was crucial that her sleuth sense start making a difference, or her friends would be forced to suffer.

Rocky was already at Abe's Deli when Gracie arrived there to meet him for lunch. The aromas of dill pickle and spicy mustard were as inviting as ever: Gracie was as at home here as she was in her own kitchen.

"Gracie!" Abe Wasserman's already large smile broadened as he came from behind the counter to give her a hug.

Rocky patted the empty stool next to his. "It's the counter today."

Gracie ordered a grilled Reuben. "Light on the dressing, Abe." She turned to her companion.

"Let's start with Cordelia," she proposed. "She seems to be at the center of everything. Could someone have some kind of grudge against her? I need to give this some thought before I go over to talk to her this afternoon."

Gracie also intended to ask her about her meeting with Comfort.

"I did do some more checking on the Jacksons," Rocky told her. "They moved here from Long Island, right after declaring bankruptcy. He ran an art gallery that dealt in antique Indonesian art. There was some question as to whether or not some of the pieces had been legally obtained."

Rocky pointed out, "If that quilt is really as unique as Comfort Harding thinks, it's probably worth a very pretty penny. The only thing is, that information was not public knowledge, and Jackson had no way of knowing about the quilt."

Abe had been listening. "It does sound like Mrs. Fountain is your best bet. She probably *isn't* your thief, but there's a good chance she knows who is. However, there's just one problem . . ."

They looked at him expectantly.

"Come on!" Rocky was impatient.

"Abe!" Gracie implored.

Abe winked. "I'm just not sure our Cordelia *knows* that she knows!"

11

COMFORT WAS SITTING AT A TABLE in the section of the library devoted to genealogy and local history when Gracie arrived. She motioned to Gracie to step outside so that they could talk. Whispering was no way to pass on a wealth of new information, that was for sure.

"I've learned a lot about Indiana history, and Willow Bend in particular. You're right, Gracie, this is a very special town. Back in the mid-19th century, they were pretty progressive, even if, locally, the abolition movement was erratic. There was also support for the Fugitive Slave Act, which obliged federal marshals to return runaways.

"Blacks suspected of being escaping slaves could be arrested without warrant and turned over to a claimant on nothing more than his sworn testimony of ownership. Without any trial. Elijah Marshall challenged this when he provided shelter to a runaway and her daughter. He was actually imprisoned and fined."

Comfort pulled out a book. "Believe it or not, not everyone in his family supported his stand. It seems that anyone who turned in people who harbored runaways was entitled to a fee, and not only that, but some people kidnapped free Blacks to sell them to slave owners. It was Elijah's own son who turned him in."

She paused. "I grew up in the seventies. I admired Martin Luther King, Jr. and idolized Rosa Parks, but I didn't know much about the ordinary folks who stood by their convictions. Gracie, I'm more proud now than ever to call Willow Bend home. Cordelia never even mentioned that an ancestor of hers was imprisoned for his anti-slavery stand."

"Speaking of Cordelia," Gracie braved, "have you ever sat down to talk to her about local history?"

"It's funny you should mention that. She called me Sunday afternoon. Charlie had been talking to her about me. I got the distinct impression she was pumping me for information."

"What kind of information?"

"Like, why did Charlie seem so taken with me? She also wanted to know whether or not I'd gotten the information from him I was looking for. I hadn't!

"I'd run into Charlie in front of Miller's Feed a couple of

days earlier, when I was picking up some fertilizer for our garden. Anyway, I told him about my project. One thing led to another and, on impulse, I offered to make a wall hanging for him."

Comfort smiled. "He's really the sweetest man. He'd heard the choir singing "Follow the Drinking Gourd," and was very touched. He knew about the North Star and our ancestors' flight to freedom, so I told him I'd make that a feature of my quilt pattern for him.

"But then, when I went to interview him, he turned reticent. I was hoping Cordelia, after I explained it all to her, could get him to talk to me on tape. But, in the end, she was just as evasive. Perhaps she's only being protective, but I suspect there's more to it."

"Like what?" Gracie wanted to know.

Comfort shrugged. "Family skeletons, I suppose." Then looking at Gracie, she asked, "Did you know the Grand Central Station of the Underground Railroad was located in Indiana, and not too far from here?"

That was also a new discovery.

"I want to get Rick to go visit the house with me. So many runaways passed through that one station! Before you arrived, I was praying. I thanked God for each and every worker on the Underground Railroad.

"I cried as I ran my finger down the list of safe houses in Indiana, and Willow Bend in particular. You can't imagine what reading about this means to an African American woman. You all cared about us before we even moved here— before we were even born. I am going to share that with Rick when we say our prayers tonight."

Gracie was touched to tears. "I don't know what to say."

"You don't have to say anything. You *live* it."

Comfort pulled out another book. "Look here. Cordelia's house is mentioned." She leaned back in her chair, and allowed Gracie to read the text. "All afternoon, I have been reading about the Marshalls and their stand against slavery. Did you know the Jacksons own the Marshall home?

"Jasper was Cordelia's grandfather's brother. There's a reason Harmon got the tourist home and Jasper the mansion."

"Cordelia told you? I had heard it, but only recently."

Comfort shook her head. "Deborah Jackson stopped by. She had a copy of a waiver Cordelia had signed as president of the Historical Society. I guess there was some dispute about whether or not Cordelia had actually signed something accepting financial responsibility for the pitcher and bowl."

Gracie was intrigued. "Cordelia was probably none too thrilled with that! What did she say?"

"She took it in stride, admitting her absentmindedness. Both of them seemed okay about the way the insurance company was handling the claim. They even chit-chatted about the upcoming tour of historical homes. That's how I learned that hers was once owned by the Marshalls."

Comfort pointed to a turn-of-the-century photograph of the Fountain house. "Deborah confessed that she'd always been curious as to why each brother inherited as they did. I was surprised when Cordelia called it poetic justice. And even moreso when she warned her to let it go at that. I swear I could hear the bones rattle in those old closets!"

"That was after Marybeth brought the quilt?"

Comfort's brow furrowed. "You think Deborah took the quilt?"

"I'm just collecting information," Gracie admitted. "It's baffling. These inherited objects seem somehow to be tied together and that's why I stopped here today. I thought I could uncover that connection."

Comfort nodded and, after a few minutes, pointed to the photograph of a black woman standing next to Cordelia's grandfather. "Nellie escaped slavery with her baby daughter and twelve-year-old brother. They crossed the Blue Ridge Mountains from Georgia by themselves. They're one of the families the Marshalls helped.

"Runaways usually could only cover a couple of miles a day, keeping just ahead of slave hunters and their dogs. It was slow going, and everwhere there were people who'd turn them in for the reward. They didn't have more than the clothes on their backs, but they followed the promise of freedom, as revealed in the quilts. The spirituals, too. They followed the North Star, the lodestone of the Drinking Gourd.

This woman and her children did it alone."

Comfort pointed to a photograph. "That's Cordelia's great-grandfather, Elijah Marshall. What a noble fellow, and how I'd love to shake his hand!"

Gracie studied the face of the man who had been such a staunch friend to so many people who had few allies they could count on. Here was a missing piece in the puzzle, she was sure of it.

How do you fit in, Elijah Marshall? You and your sons Jasper and Harmon? *Lord, do You know? Of course You do.*

"So what kind of information are you looking for now, Gracie?" Comfort asked.

Gracie took a deep breath, and explained as best she could her theory of the thefts. She told Comfort how Estelle had revealed what she'd overheard about the quilt to Marybeth. Yet, of course, she stopped short of revealing the woman's suspicion that Comfort herself had been involved in its disappearance.

"I had a feeling something was wrong with Marybeth." Comfort closed the book. "I called her to say how sorry I was to hear the quilt had been stolen. Herb answered, but he seemed cool, saying Marybeth was too busy to talk to me. Do they suspect I took it?"

Gracie grimaced.

"You know, I thought as much. I'll admit I was more than a little bothered by the fact that a white family was claiming ownership of a treasure I'm convinced has significant meaning for my own ancestors."

She met Gracie's gaze. "But I was truly sick at heart to hear that it had been stolen. Under any circumstances and no matter who was claiming it. There is a good case for the existence of such coded quilts, but no surviving prototype that shows beyond a shadow of a doubt their distinction from other quilts. Marybeth's, however, seemed to exhibit all the vaunted characteristics.

"I showed those photographs to a specialist in Ohio, and she was very excited. It seemed like we'd found proof positive! But I kept her at bay, even though she wanted to come to Willow Bend immediately. I was so excited! I know you believe me, but I was also apprehensive. I never meant to hurt Marybeth."

Gracie could only utter a heartfelt, "I know." She felt terrible that suspicion had fallen on Comfort. Now she had to solve the mystery. And time was running out.

"That's why I called you, Gracie, to get advice. I knew I had to tell Marybeth my suspicion, but taking the quilt never entered my mind. Sure, I'd like to see it in a museum, available to everybody, but that's in the future. Now is different.

"I want to work with Marybeth to discover the common thread in our histories. I hope to see her ancestor honored, along with the real creator of that quilt. That's not too much to ask, is it?"

Lord, You hear her. Her wish is so generous, and I know You will bless her for that largeness of spirit.

"Oh, Gracie, how I wanted to share this discovery with Marybeth! She seems to love quilts and history as much as I do. I don't want to steal her legacy. That quilt belongs to all of us. But, oh, how I want the true story honored and remembered!"

Gracie could only take her hand.

"I believe Marybeth really feels the same way I do," Comfort concluded. "She's just upset right now. We need to find it and determine the truth about the quilt."

12

MARGE SHOWED UP the next morning with her square for the Eternal Hope quilt. She had stitched an open Bible accented by an orange daylily, under which was written, "Consider the lilies of the field, how they grow."

"It's beautiful!" Gracie ran her hand over the gold metallic stitching on the pages of the Good Book. "Why not a daylily? Your garden is a riot of them!"

Marge sat at the table with her mug of coffee, and Gracie joined her, placing the embroidered square between them so she could continue to admire it.

"I haven't started mine," Gracie told her friend. "I need to pick a special verse to represent my spiritual life. But there are so many that are special to me."

Marge took a sip of coffee. "Okay, here's an idea—does the Bible say anything about a freezer full of delicious casseroles? Or soups?"

Gracie laughed and then, glancing at a little enamel plaque on her windowsill, saw what she needed. "'As for me and my household, we will serve the Lord.'" Isn't that the creed of every church family?

She suddenly thought of something else and explained to Marge what Abe had told her about the *Shema*. This passage from chapter six of Deuteronomy was central to the faith of all Jews, so special they embroidered it on their prayer shawls. It was the command to pass on the faith. Inscribed on parchment and kept in special protectors called *mezuzahs*, it was there on the doorposts of Jewish homes around the world.

"I even purchased one when I was in New York visiting Arlen."

"Then that's the perfect verse for you." Marge agreed. "I'm going to take my square to Comfort today. I called this morning and talked to Rick. He says she'll be home from work about four, so I thought I'd close the shop early. Maybe you could meet me at Abe's for a late lunch, and then stop over to see Comfort."

"I'm going over to the *Gazette* to do some research in their files, so that works out well with my plans. I'll be ready for a break."

"I thought Rocky was on the case. Don't tell me Scoop Gravino couldn't find anything?"

"He's had someone looking for information," Gracie told her, a bit embarrassed, "but he insists I have better sleuth sense. He thinks I'll turn up something when others can't."

"Well, Miss Marple, he's probably right."

"If only I knew what I was looking for. I have a hunch there's a historical connection, but finding that connection amid so much data is going to be next to impossible."

"I hope you do find something. This case needs to be solved soon. Suspicion around here is so thick you can practically cut the air. I've heard people say that they've decided not to lend things for fear of another theft." Marge let out an indignant *hmph*.

Over the rim of her mug, she eyed Gracie. "Jessica Larson insists that Comfort took those photos for one reason—to have some 'expert' examine them. And then it turns out the quilt is extremely valuable. Big bucks!"

The president of Eternal Hope's board was certainly efficient, Gracie gave her that. But Jessica was also more interested in money and status than most of the congregation. Trust her to project onto Comfort a motive she could understand!

Marge proceeded to unfold the whole story. It seemed Jessica had gotten to church early for the board meeting, and had answered the phone, thinking it might be her son, Jeffrey.

It turned out to be Comfort's quilt expert, who was trying to reach the owner of the unique quilt. "How she got that number I'm not certain—but it sure made Jessica's day."

Since Gracie had talked to Comfort already and heard her version, she merely nodded for Marge to go on, deciding not to share for now what she knew about the situation.

"Jessica, of course, told everyone at the meeting. Now they all have pet theories about what happened to the quilt."

Gracie was exasperated. "You probably know by now that Estelle overheard Comfort telling me her theory on the quilt. That's what she told Marybeth that got her so upset."

"Actually, there's another complication. Jessica called Marybeth before the meeting—she just had to tell her about the call from the quilt expert. Pastor Paul was livid with her but, of course, Jessica called it her duty. Marybeth admitted she'd already heard the speculation from Estelle. But she was convinced that Comfort was wrong!"

"If Estelle overheard the conversation, then it stands to reason someone else could have as well, and that someone could have been the thief. That expert told Jessica that if the photographs are any true indication, the quilt could be priceless."

Marge could hardly take it in. "This is beginning to make me dizzy!"

"That church parking lot is the original rumor mill! We should post signs that say the word *gossip* with a line slashed through!"

It was a weak joke—and, sadly, too close to the truth.

Rocky led her down the stairs to the dark, musty storage room in the basement of the *Gazette*. "They're sorted by year," he informed her. "Any references to the Marshall family are now marked. I even spent some time down here, tracking a few hunches of my own."

A lone light bulb dangled starkly above the table. "It's like looking for a dust mite in the desert," she mused out loud.

"Huh?" Rocky was staring at her.

She laughed. "Talking to myself."

"Smart and eccentric—the perfect sleuth."

"This case is baffling, so this sleuth is interested in any hunches you have, Mr. Gravino."

Rocky pulled out a box of documents. Gracie noticed the year 1861.

"Lincoln." Rocky met her gaze. "Lincoln knew what was at stake. He was my boyhood hero."

Gracie realized what she was seeing predated the *Gazette*; even newspapers had ancestors.

"Indiana was the first state to respond to President Lincoln's call to put down the rebellion. That's all they thought it was going to be at that time, a rebellion. It's sobering to realize how little they saw of what was to come. Makes you think about the decisions we're making now, and the ramifications they may have for the future."

"God understood." She smiled at him. "He alone holds the future. Belief has always been comforting to me, even though I sometimes lose perspective. God's eye is all-encompassing, though. He sees the big picture."

Rocky said gently, "You'd think a slaver would have made God angry enough to do something a long time before the Civil War!"

"God did do something."

"Look at the world, Gracie! It's a mess! What makes you think God cares? What did God do, anyway?"

She focused on a photograph of Elijah Marshall. "He gave the world men like this."

Rocky paused to consider that.

"That's Charlie Harris's great-grandmother beside him," Rocky said after a while. "Nellie Walker. Elijah Marshall purchased her freedom as well as her children's after finding them on his property drenched to the bone. Nellie survived pneumonia."

"I had a hunch the families went back several generations."

"I like hunches." He grinned. "It only dawned on me after the quilt was taken, and you pointed out they were from the same era."

Gracie grinned back.

"I put that together with some information I gleaned from that feature story I did on Cordelia's tourist home. Both houses belonged to her great-great-grandfather."

Rocky hoisted another book on the pile. "Look here." He pointed to a headline about a Negro owning property in Willow Bend. "Guess who ended up with a fat hunk of property in Elijah Marshall's will?"

"Sadie Kindness." She was enjoying being one step ahead of him. "That's how Charlie Harris ended up half-owner of Fountain's Tourist Home. I have that much figured out."

She told him what she learned from Roy Bell. "Cordelia, for all her pride, actually is tight-lipped about her history, making me think there *is* a skeleton hidden somewhere." Gracie shared Comfort's suspicion.

"Wouldn't be surprising, in that rambling old place."

"The boys would like to think the skeleton is in that tunnel." She explained Quasi's hope of unearthing a bottle with a genie inside.

Rocky perched on the edge of the table. "Now, we jump three generations, to the present, and some stolen heirlooms. How do we connect one hundred and fifty years of history?"

"That's a lot of newspapers to skim!"

"Okay, I've got one more little confounding discovery to add to the quandary. Cordelia's father's name was Harmon.

"God used Mr. Harmon to save Charlie's life—his and Meemaw's." Gracie quoted Charlie, meeting Rocky's gaze. "God woke him from a sound sleep to discover that their cabin was on fire."

Her friend shook his head.

"I'm just telling you what Charlie says."

"But who was killed when a support beam gave out in the tunnel?" Rocky opened another book. "The article doesn't come out and say it, but I have the feeling he may have been involved with the slave hunters. Two bodies were found— Harmon Marshall's and an unidentified fellow from Laurel, Georgia."

Gracie glanced at the date. "Apparently, we're back a generation."

"Ah, now for the biggest glitch! The Marshalls were not prolific progenitors. Elijah, Harmon's and Jasper's father, had only two sons. I checked. Harmon Marshall is Cordelia's grandfather. But this Harmon was twenty years old when he died—and not married. You figure that one out!"

Gracie stared at the article. "That's the same year Marybeth's great-grandmother gets married and heads west." She dug in her bag for the little journal. "The same year in which six months later the North and South would be at war!"

Lord, help me to see the link. How do this woman, Velina Ames, the quilt and the Marshalls fit together? You know everything, Lord. Please light my search.

Gracie flipped a few pages. More entries about the weather, cooking over a campfire and dust storms. No mention of Velina's husband. She flipped back to the first page. Yes, she was married. The sixth of January, 1861. Jared Ames, a forty-year-old widower.

"Happy sleuthing!" Rocky said, dusting off his hands. "I've got a staff meeting this morning. Come up and get me, and we'll have lunch."

She pulled herself away from Velina's journal. "Oh, I'm sorry, I can't. Marge and I are getting a bite later. She's closing the shop early, and we're going to see Comfort Harding."

"Poor Rick. I wonder what he makes of all this."

Gracie didn't want to get into that discussion. Besides, the journal and newspapers needed her attention. "You can join us if you want. We'll be at Abe's. I'll update you on what I learn."

"I've got a lot of work here." Rocky headed for the stairs. "You enjoy your lunch with Marge. How about I catch up with you later? Stop by your place?"

She smiled. "For supper?"

"Sixish?"

"Sounds good."

After he left, she went back to reading.

Velina was expecting a baby, that was certain. But the entries ended before her daughter's birth.

Finally, a crick in the back of her neck forced Gracie to think about quitting. It had been hours, and she hadn't learned much more. She looked at her watch. Not yet noon.

Maybe there was something in the old birth, marriage and death registers kept in the genealogy section of the library. That seemed a good next step. She'd have time to stop by.

Outside the reading room, Gracie was waylaid by Deborah Jackson returning some books.

"How is Charlie?" Deborah wanted to know.

Gracie was ashamed to admit that she hadn't yet checked on the man. That was another stop she'd have to make before heading home later. Thank goodness she'd taken a casserole out of the freezer! Uncle Miltie could pop it in the oven. "I hope to get over there this afternoon," she told Deborah.

"Gracie, I do want to apologize for my husband's less-than-cordial welcome the other day." Deborah lowered her gaze. "Carl's made a few bad investments. He'd be angry if he knew I was telling you this, but I sensed. . . ."

"I'd like to be your friend," Gracie assured her.

A warm smile. "Are you looking for a book?"

Gracie laughed. "I've got four mysteries piled by my bed. And last time I was in, I took out a history of Willow Bend. No, I have enough reading to last me a month of Sundays!"

"I like mysteries," Deborah said. "Especially cozies. I go through them like candy."

They exchanged the names of favorite authors. "If only real-life mysteries were as predictable," Gracie complained.

"I like figuring things out—particularly people. I guess that's why I find mysteries so appealing."

Lord, what are You trying to show me here? Is it something about Deborah? I know she needs a friend. Is that it? You want me to confide in her? Share this mystery?

"I'm doing a little research," Gracie explained. "I'd really like to figure out who took the missing heirlooms. We all need to know, really."

Deborah held Gracie's gaze. "I know people think Carl or I did it. Herb Bower implied as much. Gracie, I *did* have the opportunity. I think you should know that I was at the opening reception. I came and went without anyone noticing—no one said as much as, 'Hello, how are you?'"

And, looking at Gracie once again, "Not that I expected them to. Because I know I seem standoffish. I'm really just shy, though."

"Phyllis says you're wonderful with difficult patients," Gracie remembered. "You're not shy then."

"I love taking care of people." Deborah's eyes brightened. "When patients need me, I guess I forget myself. I just want to help them heal." Gracie regarded her intently.

Deborah's expression turned serious again. "I'll be frank, Gracie. Carl never really liked that pitcher and bowl. They weren't his taste at all. I think secretly he's glad they were stolen. The money's more attractive to him, for sure, but that doesn't make him the thief."

"Thank you for telling me that. I think the quilt and the pitcher set have something in common. If I could only figure out what it is, we might find the thief."

Gracie now revealed what she'd already gleaned from the

newspaper archives. Deborah offered to help her now, and in less than an hour they'd made some progress. But Gracie realized it would take a genealogy buff to sort out all the Harmons. They also discovered Cordelia's father, Harmon, had married one Sarah Post in 1905, and that while his father was at the wedding, his mother was listed as deceased.

GRACIE TOYED WITH THE cottage cheese and fruit on her plate, trying to keep her mind on what Marge was saying, but snippets of historical data kept darting in front of the conversation.

She couldn't figure out the Harmons. And what did all that history have in common with the missing items almost one hundred fifty years later?

"Earth to Gracie." Marge was staring at her.

"Is there something wrong with your salad?" Abe wanted to know.

"It's wonderful, Abe." She took a bite. "I'm just a bit pre-occupied, that's all."

"I should have asked you straight off," Marge said. "What did you uncover in the newspaper archives?"

Abe went to wait on another customer.

Gracie reported the bits of information, reading them from

her note pad in order of importance. Abe stopped every now and then to look at the list and ask a question.

"It seems to me, what all this leads to to is the fact Mrs. Fountain must be involved somehow," Abe concluded. "After all, this is her family history."

As much as she hated to admit it, that *was* what it looked like.

"Perhaps someone has a score to settle," Abe suggested.

Marge couldn't resist, "Hey, maybe someone from Avery!"

Abe furrowed his brow, and Marge explained the joke.

"Seriously," she went on, "Cordelia is not only the head of the Founders' Day program, but president of the Historical Society as well. She's involved with the Daughters of the American Revolution, and you know they take their pedigrees seriously. Maybe she denied membership to someone."

"But why these two heirlooms?" Gracie wanted to know.

"Nothing else has been taken, right?" Abe said.

Marge agreed. "That's easy. It's because now they have everything else under lock and key. Something we obviously should have done from the beginning."

Abe stroked his chin. "Perhaps one theft is a cover-up for the other—a red herring, of sorts. Maybe someone is trying to throw you off the trail! I've seen similar plot twists in movies."

"I've thought of that, too," Gracie told him, "especially considering the potential value of the quilt."

"But the truth is, either could be the targeted heirloom.

What they both have in common is the Marshall family, and that's just too coincidental to ignore."

"We don't really have a quilt connection," Marge reminded her. "Unless the quilt was made by the African American— what was her name?"

"Nellie Walker." *That had to be it!* "But how did Velina Ames end up with it?"

"That's your department, Sherlock," Marge told her.

Gracie said to Marge. "Well, then, we have clues to collect, Watson!"

Abe's eyes lit up. "That reminds me of a joke I heard the other day. I'm going to tell it to your uncle, but I'll try it out on you first, okay?"

"Holmes and Watson were lying out under the night sky. 'The stars are beautiful,' says Watson. 'Why, yes, they are,' says Holmes, 'but what do they tell you, Watson?' 'I don't know, Holmes,' says the assistant."

Abe grinned, waiting a moment to reveal the punch line. "'They tell me that someone stole our tent!'"

"Uncle Miltie will love it!"

Marge rolled her eyes, but laughed. "Two comedians are more than Willow Bend can handle."

"Vaudeville may still come back someday, you know," Abe reminded them. "The way they're bringing back the old things, anything could happen. Your uncle and I will be ready!"

Rick showed Gracie and Marge in to where Comfort and Lillian were sitting on the floor by the fireplace with paper dolls spread out all around them.

"Paper dolls!" Marge exclaimed. "I haven't seen any for years!"

Lillian looked at them sweetly.

Comfort stood up.

"We don't want to take up a lot of your time," Marge said, retrieving her quilt square from her pocketbook.

Comfort admired it. She told them that, so far, more than a dozen families had turned in their pieces. "I suppose more will come in the week after next. That's the deadline."

"Speaking of quilts," Gracie began, "do you know that your expert contacted the church?"

Comfort nodded. "So does Marybeth."

"We know," Gracie said.

Comfort moved to the couch beside Marge. "We had a long talk. I told her that it broke my heart to see such a treasured heirloom disappear.

"We have much in common. We love quilts and family history. She wants the truth known as much as I do. Marybeth even agreed to have the experts look at it, if she ever gets it back. We actually had a lovely visit.

"But I still feel bad, because she remains convinced the quilt was made by her great-great-grandmother."

"And you're positive it wasn't?" This was Marge. "Couldn't her ancestor have been involved with the Underground Railroad?"

Comfort admitted that, yes, it was a possibility. Yet Gracie understood that Marybeth was right: this woman longed to have her oral tradition confirmed by the quilt with the knots that had first caught her attention.

"We don't have the quilt now, but let me try to show you what it was that I saw." Comfort stood to retrieve the photographs from the drawer in the end table, then sat down between Gracie and Marge.

"At first glance, this use of recycled fabric would seem the practical choice for pioneers. But Velina was not poor—most pioneers weren't. It took money for a trip like that. The women brought material especially for making quilts. They didn't want to put hours of work into a coverlet made of worn pieces that would be threadbare in a few washings."

Gracie remembered the entry in Velina's diary. "But they would use remnant bits of special garments, right?"

"Oh, yes, of course. And there were scrap quilts, and crazy quilts. But this is rather complicated, with the center panel and embroidered sashing."

Comfort retrieved a photograph. "They would have used a better quality backing." She pointed to the picture of the back side of the quilt. "This backing was pieced from a variety of muslin, all in varying stages of wear."

She looked at Gracie. "That's why I was running my hand over the back of the quilt. I was trying to determine the wear. I don't believe it went through many washings. The fabrics were old to begin with."

Marge studied that snapshot. "That doesn't really prove anything. I mean, it's got to be pretty hard to pinpoint the creator of a quilt by the type of fabric that was used."

"You're right." Comfort scooted closer. "That was only one clue. Now, look at the knotting. It's in hemp. Not only is it cheap cord, but it's eye-catching."

She smiled knowingly. "Eye-catching to a runaway needing to know how many more miles between stations on the Underground Railroad."

Gracie moved closer, too. "You said something about the choice of patterns? That they were symbols and road markers?"

"Yes, it was the Quilt Code," Comfort said simply. "That's what we call it. This particular one's a sampler, most often used to teach the craft, but I believe it's also a mnemonic device, for remembering the code. Marybeth's quilt utilizes all the known symbols. The patterns seem to appear in story order: Monkey Wrench, Wagon Wheel, Flying Geese, Bear Claw, Drunkard's Path, Cathedral, Crossroads, Bow Ties and Log Cabin."

They studied the photographs as Comfort explained that the Monkey Wrench meant the leader was ready, and they should start to gather the tools, both the material things they owned and mental tools like cunning. The Wagon Wheel told them to pack only what was absolutely essential, and to understand that they were leaving everything they knew, forever. Flying Geese told them to take their cue from the migrating birds.

The Bear Claw was the path through the mountains, and they were to zig-zag (Drunkard's Path). Cathedral represented the caves where they were to hide. Crossroads was easy. Comfort reminded Gracie that Cleveland was literally the crossroads for the Underground Railroad. Bow Ties could be angled to represent morning, midday, evening and night. The Log Cabin would have been a safe house.

She pointed to the center design. "Notice the North Star in the middle—the lead star in the constellation Drinking Gourd, as the Big Dipper was known to slaves."

"Look at what this artist did." They followed Comfort's finger out from the center. "See the mountains and rivers? These are icons for hope. Follow the North Star through the mountains—to Canada and freedom."

Comfort paused. "Someone created this quilt to keep the story alive. This one was probably not hung on a fence, but created for a child, or a grandchild—their legacy to remember the journey."

"Wow." Marge held the photograph closer. "All that, stitched in a blanket! Amazing."

Their friend nodded. "Marybeth thought so, too, when I explained it. As much as she wants that quilt to be part of her family history, she could see what I saw when I showed her the snapshots."

"I can't believe I never heard of the Code before!" Gracie told Comfort. "My mother and grandmother liked to quilt."

"Books are just starting to come out on the subject," Comfort said. "The oral tradition has been around, and we know the spirituals were used to relay music codes. It's all hard to prove, however, and a concept like coding makes it doubly difficult. These stories have been passed down but never validated until recently.

"The woman who called the church asking about the quilt is the author of a book on the subject. To actually see and touch one of these quilts would be a dream come true for her, so I can't blame her for doing what she did. I know that holding the quilt on my lap was quite an experience for me. Imagine, actually touching something that helped change your destiny—the destiny of your people!"

Comfort picked out another photograph. "Look at what's in the background in this snapshot. A sign with the name of our church."

"So that's how she found out the phone number."

Comfort nodded. "Let your fingers do the walking. She probably was on to directory assistance before you could say boo. But, because of that, now I'm a suspect."

"If it's any comfort, Gracie and I don't believe you took it," Marge said. "It was pure coincidence, you being at Cordelia's that afternoon. Deborah was there, too."

Marge turned to Gracie. "We've got to figure this out! Herb's a fine officer of the law, but this isn't your typical crime. It's about history and people! We have to talk to Cordelia again."

"I'd like to talk to Charlie again, too," Comfort said. "But I don't think Cordelia wants anyone doing that. She wants to protect him, even when he doesn't seem to need it. The time I caught up with him at Hammie's store, he was happy to tell me about his grandmother."

Gracie agreed. "He's always more than happy to talk about his Meemaw, it seems."

"She was born a slave," Comfort said. "Imagine that! Charlie is one generation removed from slavery. I've got to write his story."

Gracie flipped through the pictures again. Could this quilt have been Nellie Walker's? But what about Velina Ames? And who wanted it enough now to steal it?

Gracie glanced at her watch. She still had a lot to do before supper. It would be nice to have a special dessert. But could she get home in time to service Rocky's sweet tooth?

"I'm sure no one really suspects you, Comfort. Unfortunately, when something like this happens, emotion often overrides common sense."

"I hope you're right." Comfort sighed.

"Don't you worry, Gracie and I are going to solve this case, if Herb can't." Marge looked confident.

"Lord," Gracie began, and they all bowed their heads. "Thank You for giving us one another. Help all of us to believe in each other, and to maintain forgiving spirits. Tame any tongue tempted to gossip.

"And make sure any important gossip doesn't escape our attention. It's better to *know* thy enemy."

"Amen," they said as one.

TWO MESSAGES WERE ON her answering machine. The first was a reminder from Barb Jennings that there was a community choir practice scheduled at Waxman Tabernacle. The second was from Deborah Jackson. Gracie hit "Replay."

". . . Carl has been arrested. We're at the police station. They won't tell me anything. Please come as soon as possible!" Gracie turned right around.

Jim Thompson greeted her. "You can't go in. The chief's talking to Jackson."

"Gracie!" Deborah sprang from her chair nearby.

They hugged. "What's going on, Jim?"

"You understand I can't tell you, ma'am."

Gracie decided diplomacy was best. "Jim, I know *you* understand how upset police stations make honest citizens.

Doesn't Mrs. Jackson have a right to know what you're holding her husband for? What crime he has committed?"

"I have my orders, Gracie. If you want to have a seat, I'll tell the chief you're here."

Jim was in her Sunday school class. He could be a bit professionally overzealous, that was true; but when the time came he also knew how to be a friend to the friendless. Carl and Deborah really were in good hands. Gracie smiled and thanked him, reminding herself he was only doing his job.

She turned to Deborah. "You honestly don't have any idea what's going on?"

"Someone from the county sheriff's office came by this morning with a warrant. I told him Carl was in Chicago on business, but he knew differently. In fact, he was up in the studio apartment—I just wasn't aware he'd come home. Carl wouldn't even look at me when the officer escorted him to his car. He called out for me to get him a lawyer. Next thing I knew, he was headed down our street in a police car."

"Did you?"

She nodded. "The attorney for whom I'd left a message called back a little while ago. I heard Officer Thompson put the call through to where they have Carl." She looked at Gracie sadly.

Lord, fill me with Your peace, so I can be of help here. I know You are in control. Please give me wisdom—words of comfort and encouragement.

"I've been praying since I got here," Deborah confided. "Lately, I've had a feeling that Carl was in some kind of trouble. It's been too painful to think about, really. He's never an easy man to live with, but these days . . . I just don't know what to expect."

She lowered her head, and Gracie felt her sobs. "I've thought about divorcing him. Our marriage hasn't been good for a long time, but it was tolerable, and I stayed for the kids. But our youngest has been gone for almost five years. Now, I don't know why I put up with it." She shuddered.

"No, that's not true. I stay because I remember the man I married. It was after Carl started to get successful that things changed. He just was never happy, no matter how much he earned."

She once again began touching her finger where a wedding ring had once been. Such disappointment! Gracie's own experience had been so different—what if this had been her lot? It was agony to contemplate.

"I do care for him, Gracie," she said. "But he's so insecure, and so convinced money and prestige will change our lives for the better—even though it never does. It's only an illusion.

"I didn't say anything when he invested Aunt Aggie's money in this latest venture, buying and selling collectibles on speculation on the Internet. I just wanted him to be happy. I had my work . . . and the children, too, but what will I tell *them*?"

Jim appeared in front of them. "The chief will see you now."

Deborah stood. "What about my husband? When can I see him?"

"A detective from Chicago PD is en route. They're going to have a lot of questions, and may want to take him back to the city. But, ma'am, I think you'll have a little time with him before they arrive." His expression was kind. "I'll check on that, and see what I can arrange. And, ma'am, I'm really sorry I can't tell you more."

Gracie stood beside her friend. "Well, let's see Herb."

"Gracie," Jim implored. "You know as well as I do that Herb will not be able to tell you any particulars. Carl's not making it easier—he refuses to talk to us until he has an attorney, and that doesn't look like it's going to happen for the time being."

"This isn't about the pitcher and bowl?" Gracie ventured.

Jim shook his head. "No, it's a lot more serious."

"Gracie, if you don't mind, I think I'd rather go in there alone. The important thing is for me to see Carl, and it might anger him to know I involved you." Deborah's expression was now apologetic. "But, please, continue to pray."

"Why don't I call Ann McNeil?" She explained to Deborah that the attorney was a dear friend, and because she was local, she might be able to come right away. "If Carl wants the other firm, that can be his decision. But at least for now, he'll have counsel."

Deborah wasn't certain this was a good idea. "Why would she want to help us? We're the ones who entered the suit against your church, and the town."

"Gracie," Jim pleaded. "I think she should ask Carl what he wants first. He's facing some pretty serious charges, so he might just need that high-powered counsel."

Fifteen minutes hadn't passed before Herb himself brought Deborah Jackson back to the waiting area. "Carl would like to see Mrs. McNeil, if you wouldn't mind making the call."

She pulled out her cell phone and called Ann, who agreed to come immediately. In the meantime, Gracie made small talk. "How's Marybeth?"

He looked uncomfortable, avoiding her gaze. "As well as can be expected, under the circumstances. Looks like we're not any closer to recovering her quilt."

"She seemed in better spirits when I left her."

"I think we'll all rest easier when we apprehend this thief."

"Are there new leads?" Gracie wanted to know.

"I can't discuss it."

Herb often talked over cases with her, saying that he valued her input. But something was very different this time. For once, they did not seem to be on the same side of the fence.

When Ann arrived, some facts quickly became evident.

"Carl is alleged to have sold a stolen signed Tiffany vase," Deborah said in a low voice.

Gracie was startled. Everyone knew how collectible Tiffany glass was.

Deborah continued, "A very expensive piece, and unique. The previous owner not only had it insured, but there are lots of photographs of it. I remember when he got the piece. He was ecstatic, saying the seller had no idea what she had. Turns out she did, though. It looks like this little old lady was actually the fence for a ring of burglars."

Deborah laughed. "Ironic, isn't it? He paid the woman cash! She insisted, of course. He even used money he owed to someone else. Then that fellow wanted to be paid immediately, but Carl hadn't yet found a buyer for the Tiffany vase.

Luckily for him, the theft of the pitcher set gave him a way out. The insurance company paid promptly."

"Let me talk to him," Ann said.

"What are you going to do now?" Gracie asked Deborah.

"Call my son in Chicago. If the police take Carl there, I can stay with Scott."

Gracie was glad to hear Deborah would have the support of her son. It made her think of Arlen. She resolved to call him as soon as she got home.

"Carl was scared to ask me to stay," Deborah was saying. "He knows I have every reason to wash my hands of him. He looked just like a frightened little boy in there. I can't desert him, not now.

"I'm probably crazy to remain, but a vow is a vow. I owe it to myself to honor my commitment to Carl, and to God to honor the vows we shared in His presence."

Gracie's eyes glistened. "Healing takes time."

Deborah acknowledged the truth in that familiar phrase.

"But it's love, not time, that truly heals all wounds," Gracie continued. "Loving him will be tough sometimes. He's got an ordeal in front of him. But remember, God can love him for you, when you can't. When I'd get upset with El, I'd ask the Lord to love him for me, because at that moment I wanted to strangle that man. God would open my heart and I just couldn't stay mad."

She smiled gently. "Deborah, my dear, I'll be praying for you."

"Thank you, Gracie."

Rocky's little black sedan swung into the space next to Fannie Mae at the police station. Gracie waited for her friend to emerge. "Heard that the Chicago police are picking up a suspect in a series of high-end burglaries. Some smuggling across state lines may have been involved. Could be a case for the FBI." He looked rumpled.

"Good luck getting Herb to tell you anything more than that!"

"So, how did you scoop me, anyway?"

"Deborah called me. She needed moral support."

"You're amazing, Gracie Lynn Parks!"

She accepted his admiration, but insisted she was only being a Christian. If Deborah needed her, then Gracie was on call. The Lord's emergency service, you might say.

"I guess I better talk to Herb, out of journalistic duty."

He thought a moment. "I would have liked Carl Jackson to be our man. As it is now, I'm really just doing catch-up, so this case doesn't get ahead of me. Herb, also, is more likely to talk to me off the record than any reporter I send over."

Gracie was getting into her car when he called, "What's for dessert?"

Gracie let herself laugh. "You can pick up a half-gallon of French vanilla ice cream, since it looks like I'm not going to have time to get fancier than opening a jar of hot fudge sauce!"

Uncle Miltie had set the dinner table and, practically beside himself with excitement, told Gracie that the local chapter of the Veterans of Foreign Wars had asked him to lead them on Founders' Day.

"Not many us left, you know. There are lots of veterans of Korea and Vietnam, but not the guys who served in the Big One."

Gracie listened as she lit the candles. She was sobered by the reminder of his age, and what the consequence might be of putting off the interview with him she'd been meaning to do for some time now.

George Morgan had not only survived active service, but had been a prisoner of war, something he was usually reluctant to talk about. He was a decorated war hero. It was up to her to record his story; she owed him that for his steadfast devotion to her and for the way his arrival in her household had brought much-needed cheer to her life.

She owed it to posterity, too.

"I've always wanted to ride in a red convertible, flanked by pretty beauty queens. Especially when they're as cute as that girl who won Dairy Princess."

Gracie shook her head. "You're incorrigible."

"Keeps me young." His eyes sparkled.

"Looks like everything is going ahead as planned for Founders' Day," she told him. "I was afraid, in light of what's happened, that there would be a shadow over the festivities."

"Folks are upset about the thefts, sure, but that doesn't have to put a damper on our achievements. We've got a lot to celebrate. Why, haven't I always said that the Lord made Willow Bend paradise on earth? And that fact alone is worth a pretty big shindig."

Rocky arrived just in time to sit down for dinner, praising the meal before she even got the casserole out of the oven. She had him trained, all right. Gracie smiled, as both her menfolk asked for second helpings.

"You were right about Herb and the Jackson case, Gracie," Rocky told her. "They're pretty tight-lipped down at the station."

Uncle Miltie's interest was piqued. "So, they've fixed on Jackson again?"

Gracie explained. "It's not that simple. Deborah phoned a little while ago to tell me the Chicago detectives questioned Carl, then released him on his own recognizance.

"Of course, he can't leave town, and needs to stay available for questioning. He's going to be charged with receiving stolen goods, and will have to stand trial. It's going to be hard on his family."

"Well, Deborah Jackson may no longer be a suspect." Rocky's tone was impatient. "But that doesn't eliminate our suspects among the Eternal Hope clean-up crew, or Cordelia Fountain—or Comfort Harding, for that matter."

Gracie eyed him. "Or a person we haven't even considered yet."

"And who haven't we considered?" He stared.

She shrugged. "We just don't have any real evidence implicating any of those people you mentioned. We need to dig deeper, that's all."

However, what past and present coincidences had come to light did seem to point to another suspect—one whose identity she was not quite ready to reveal.

15

THE NEW ROBES ARRIVED with great fanfare. Barb invited Pastor Paul to offer a blessing, like the ones they did whenever a member moved into a new home. Gracie couldn't think of a better way to set up housekeeping. She was proud of Barb for suggesting they do the same with the choir robes. They would also offer thanks to their anonymous benefactor by asked a blessing for him—or her— as well.

Rick Harding had brought his new digital camera to record the event for their Web page. He was full of ideas for developing Eternal Hope's sanctum in cyberspace!

Gracie had been quite impressed with what Rick previewed for them on the church computer. Rick had even sent Arlen the link, which he said would make Eternal Hope only a mouse click away from New York. Gracie had to admit the gadget did vaguely resemble the rodent for which it was named. She could just see Gooseberry hunting it down, and how disappointed he'd be when he caught it.

Arlen had been trying to convince her to buy a computer, claiming e-mail was not only instant, but inexpensive. If he couldn't talk her into something any other way, he always was canny enough to try the savings angle!

Suddenly she recognized that Estelle and Barb were arguing. "It's too tight! Are you sure you ordered the right size?"

Barb crossed her arms. "I ordered exactly the size you told me. Remember, you insisted on a smaller size than the chart recommended. I told you it was going to be tight across your shoulders and chest!"

"Well, my old robe was the same size, and it fit perfectly!" Estelle complained.

"Estelle, please!" Barb was not hiding her impatience. "I can send this back and order one in a bigger size."

"I do not need a *bigger* size! If you hadn't ordered from such a *cheap* company, it would fit properly."

Barb threw her hands up in despair. "Let's hope they can get a bigger size here before the concert. The large sizes are specially made." And, glaring at Estelle. "They're more expensive, too!"

"You're not paying for them," Estelle pointed out.

Marge had a diplomatic intervention to offer. "Is it really

that tight? I mean, they seem to be plenty large in the body—couldn't the shoulders be altered? Maybe we could just have someone alter it."

"Clothes used to be made to fit! Now they make everything in countries where everyone's a midget. It's ridiculous. I tell you I ordered the same size as my old gown."

Barb pursed her lips. "You're forgetting how old it was, I guess. Or how old you've gotten. I guess they were a bit more generous with the fabrics in those days."

Lester Twomley laughed. "Seems to me, as models got skinnier, the people they modeled the clothes for got heavier!"

Estelle continued to fume.

Don Delano offered to trade gowns. He was a good six feet tall, and broad across the shoulders. A big man, but not overweight. Women considered the bachelor chemistry teacher quite handsome. Gracie remembered her niece, Carter Stephens, had found him attractive. Now he was turning his boyish charm on their stubborn diva.

"Men's gowns usually run fuller," he pointed out. "I stand in the back, so it wouldn't matter if we trade and yours is a little short on me."

"I'd be happy to hem Don's," Marybeth offered. She smiled at Estelle. "Here, let me help you."

Gracie felt humble. Marybeth's graciousness to Estelle was proof positive that theirs was a forgiving family. God's children. "'They have their Father's eyes,'" she whispered, recalling a line from a favorite song."

"*Hmm?*" It was Rick beside her.

"I was just thanking God for this bunch. It's wonderful, really, how we always seem to work out our problems once we put our minds—and hearts—to it."

"Comfort has really appreciated your friendship, Gracie. She's been understandably unnerved by the circumstances, and the support of her church means a lot. She didn't grow up in the church, but felt called to try a Christian fellowship when we were in college. She was lonely, and having some trouble with her parents."

He smiled. "That's where I met her. She was so gorgeous, I was just bowled over. She was into her African roots, and wore those beautiful head wraps and gowns. That kind of scared me off at first. But she was so smart . . . and interesting. I got up my courage to ask her to a concert—even picked up a bouquet of flowers for the event."

Gracie was fascinated. She loved knowing how couples had first met.

"Anyway, when I got to her apartment, I decided the flowers were overdoing it, and that she'd probably take them wrong, figuring I was trying to put the moves on her. I tossed them in the back seat of the car, and almost forgot about them."

Rick turned to face Gracie. "But that night, despite all my uncertainties, I knew I was going to marry her. Still, it took three years, and quite a few more bouquets, to convince her. But she still has some petals from that first bunch pressed into our Bible."

"I'm so glad you came to Willow Bend," Gracie told him.

"So are we. Thanks again for standing behind Comfort. It means a lot to her, Gracie—your faith in us is like a shining light. It brightens everything."

"Mrs. Parks?" It was Chuckie Moon calling her on her cell phone.

Gracie pulled Fannie Mae off the road in order to talk to him.

"We just found something totally cool!"

"Where are you?"

"The basement of the tourist home. We found some kind of code on the wall! Mrs. Fountain isn't here. She unlocked the cellar doors for us before she left, so you'll have to come in that way. By the way, Amy Cantrell's here, with Francine Barton. They wanted to see the tunnel."

That worried Gracie. "Does Mrs. Fountain know?"

"Sure! Pastor Paul was here earlier with a couple of the kids. Amy and Francine stayed. We've got this place looking great! We're going to go to Martin's when we're done here."

She could hear Quasi in the background. "Tell her to hurry."

By the time Gracie arrived, Cordelia had come back and was in the tunnel with the kids. On the foundation stone were simply-etched drawings of the Big Dipper, a river, mountains and also a house with a heart in the middle.

"Mrs. Fountain thinks the runaway slaves drew them while they were waiting for safe passage." Francine said. "We want to clean them up, and we can do it carefully."

Gracie glanced at Cordelia. Did Gracie detect some slight discomfort there? Her blue eyes were unblinking, but, nonetheless, Gracie felt her wariness.

"It's not safe way back there!" Cordelia warned. "That's where the tunnel collapsed. We're actually under the inside of the house right now. That was dug by hand and braced with log beams, but that was almost two hundred years ago."

Cordelia moved to stand beside Gracie at the barricaded opening. "It used to get water in the spring that flooded into the basement more than a few times. It's probably turned into a haven for squirrels and mice and who knows what else! There's not been anyone back there for as long as I can remember."

She looked at the teenagers. "I don't want anyone back there. Chuckie, you can put in those joists you were asking me about, but only in this area. I'll talk to Roy Bell about rigging up a light. This is far enough for anyone to come to appreciate the tunnel."

"There's nothing back there but splintered wood, rocks and dirt, anyway," Quasi confirmed.

Amy crouched to peek between the boards. "There could be more drawings. Isn't anybody curious?"

"You know what killed the cat, Miss Cantrell," Cordelia reminded her. "Mind my warning! That should be all I have to say!"

Gracie turned back to the etchings. "This is a historical treasure, Cordelia. Comfort Harding and I were reading about your grandfather. He was quite a man."

"Actually, this tunnel ran between two dwellings. A caretaker's home was between the main house and the creek. That house burned in the twenties, however."

"Charlie will be curious about what we've been doing. So be sure you're polite to him." She led the way back upstairs.

"He's not such a bad old guy," Martin said. "I've seen the way he watches everything. There's security for you, Mrs. Fountain."

"Yeah, we couldn't pull anything over on that guy," Quasi said. He looked at Cordelia. "No offense, Mrs. Fountain, but your cat would still be in that mailbox if he hadn't seen us."

Cordelia looked triumphant. "I knew it, I knew it!"

Chuckie stepped forward with an eye to damage-control. "We're really sorry, ma'am. It was a stupid stunt, and we were just kids then."

"Dumb middle-schoolers," Quasi corrected him.

Chuckie squirmed, glancing at Amy.

"You put her cat in a mailbox?" Amy stared at Chuckie.

"Yuck!" Francine stepped back and eyed Martin. "And to think we were going to have ice cream with catnappers!"

"Oh, come on, lighten up," Quasi said. "It was a stupid prank. And the cat's none the worse for the little vacation. Besides, it was a long time ago!"

Martin elbowed Quasi. "We were going to ring your bell, Mrs. Fountain, but Mr. Harris came out of nowhere. If looks could kill, we wouldn't be standing here today owning up to that stupid prank."

"We couldn't be sure what he would do to us if he caught us," Quasi went on. "In those days we thought you were a witch—"

Martin headlocked him, covering Quasi's mouth while trying to look suavely confident. No easy feat. "But now we know different, don't we?" He glared at Quasi.

"I think I might have some ginger cookies," Cordelia changed the subject, effectively burying the hatchet. Gracie was impressed . . . and amazed.

Gracie followed Martin upstairs. "You guys ought to go into politics or maybe show business! Wow!"

"How about law enforcement?" He grinned.

"You'll make captain in no time!"

"My mother used to conduct school, right here at this very table," Cordelia told them as she poured minty iced tea.

"And Charlie was her best pupil. I would get mad when Charlie recited the multiplication tables faster, and he would have to slow down and wait for my response. You could never predict what he would excel at and where he would stumble."

"How is he?" Gracie asked, feeling guilty for not asking about him sooner. She hated to admit that she'd become obsessed with what seemed like a puzzle in patchwork.

Gracie sensed her hostess's guard go up. "I haven't seen him much lately. With all the time he's putting in at Hammie Miller's, he's exhausted when he comes home. He's been taking his supper to his room."

Cordelia met her gaze. "I'm sure you've noticed that he's not one for socializing."

Gracie remembered how she'd enjoyed his memories of his grandmother and her singing them through the tragedy of the fire. Cordelia, though, was clearly not receptive to any discussion about Charlie that she didn't control.

W HEN GRACIE STOPPED BY Cordelia's house the next day looking for Charlie, she found Martin and Quasi carrying debris out of the cellar.

"Is Mr. Harris around?" she called.

"He was here, but I think he left a while ago. Mrs. Fountain had one of her meetings." Then dusting his hands, he glanced back toward the cellarway. "She won't be back until, oh, probably dark."

Martin added, "We're just finishing up for the afternoon."

"I think I'll just check on your progress." She started down the stairs when Amy crossed the threshold.

"Oh! Oh . . . hi!!" The girl flashed an odd grin.

Chuckie appeared right behind her. "We're almost finished for the day," he said. He glanced at Amy.

"I was helping Charles. I swept out the tunnel." She gave a nervous giggle. "I guess I must look a fright."

Gracie nodded, trying not to laugh. Chuckie blushed a bright shade of lobster, plainly embarrassed that Gracie might suspect a budding romance. But it was either that, or something else was going on. What, though?

"You folks want to show me around?" Gracie said lightly.

Chuckie and Amy backed down into the cellar to let her come in. "I rigged this light up so we could see to clean those etchings. It's going to look really nice. You want to see?"

Gracie played it cool.

"Okay, okay, we were snooping. We were back where we weren't supposed to be."

"I put him up to it," Amy confessed. "I think secret tunnels are just awesome. So do we all."

"If that tunnel gives way," Gracie warned, "you're going to regret it, Amy. And if you escape death by burial, Cordelia surely will kill you when she finds out you've disobeyed her!"

"You're not going to tell on us, are you?" It was Quasi behind her.

From the depths of the tunnel came Francine. "Hurry, you guys, I can see light!" She stopped short, spotting Gracie. "Uh-oh!"

Gracie looked sternly at her. "You're right about that!"

"We found where the tunnel opens up, but there are tons of rocks blocking it," Francine told her.

Quasi turned to head back in

"Halt!" Gracie called a minute too late, as he disappeared from view.

"It's okay, Mrs. Parks," Martin told her. He pointed to shiny black joists gracing the tunnel's entrance. "We've got it braced."

Chuckie nodded. "It's safe."

"Even if it's still spooky!" Francine added.

Gracie wasn't satisfied it was safe, but Quasi's voice echoed out for them to follow. Gracie grabbed a flashlight.

At the entrance she turned and put on her most furious glare. "The rest of you stay here! You got that? Don't move an inch!"

They nodded.

Making her way through the opening slowly, Gracie finally emerged on the other side. There she had to duck and pull in her shoulders. It was dank and moldy, the air on her skin making goosebumps. She was tempted to turn around, but—

"Hurry up!" Quasi motioned with his flashlight to a pile of rocks blocking what did look like a doorway. When she drew near, he shone the flashlight through an opening. "This is too cool! There's a doorway on the other side, and a room, too!"

He stuck his hand through the cavity to shine light into the recesses. "This place has got to be the best secret hide-away ever!"

She strained to see, but couldn't make out anything but a thick hand-hewn log joist.

Quasi told her their theory. "We figure someone filled in that opening. It wasn't part of the collapse, because this section of the tunnel is intact."

Gracie shone her own light through the hole. "This must be the caretaker's house Cordelia told us about."

"Probably."

"Did you guys try to find the opening on the other side?"

"No luck."

He grinned. "We just discovered this. We were hauling out the first loads of stone when you showed up."

"Cordelia is going to be livid!"

"Not if you don't tell her," he pointed out. "We were planning to put everything back the way we found it."

When they got back to the cellar, Gracie repeated the ban on reentering the tunnel, warning them that she was going to have to inform Cordelia.

"Just don't tell Mr. Harris," Quasi pleaded. "Please. He might not understand we didn't mean any harm."

After Gracie had sent the kids home, she couldn't resist doing a little outside exploring of her own. She walked along what seemed to be the perimeter of the old caretaker's house's foundation. There was a stone wall at the far edge of Cordelia's property which could have been part of another dwelling.

Gracie glanced down at her already grubby knit pants and dirty sneakers. Fashionable Marge made fun of her preference for comfort over style, but this afternoon, she was glad she'd stuck with practicality. On closer inspection of the border, she discovered vestiges of an old footpath.

"Mrs. Parks!"

She turned to see Quasi racing to meet her. "What are you doing back here?"

He straightened indignantly. "Nosing around, just like you!"

She stepped in front of the path.

Quasi looked beyond her. "Wow, you think it leads to an outside entrance to that room?"

"I thought you were going for ice cream," she said, trying to redirect his focus.

"You heard three's a crowd—well, five is the same. The girls went home to clean up before going to The Sweet Shoppe."

He grinned. "I like the idea of adventure. I figured you'd already be blabbing to Mrs. Fountain. Then we'd never get to set foot on her property again. So it was now or never to check out the black dungeon at the end of the tunnel."

Gracie stared. She longed to think of an excuse for sending the boy packing. But there was no way around it—his agility would be handy in navigating the tricky entrance. If, indeed, there was another way in, at all. Technically, they were trespassing, and she couldn't in good conscience make the boy accessory to a crime. But once again, before she had a chance to intercept him, he went barreling ahead.

"Might be snakes!" He turned around to face her. "I'll scout it out for you, Mrs. P. They say there are rattlers in the rocks creekside, and on a sunny afternoon they come out to sunbathe."

She shuddered at the thought, hoping he was just saying that to scare her.

"The path dead-ends in overgrowth!" Quasi called over his shoulder. "I'll have to clear it for you."

"Quasi, we're going to get in trouble!"

"Mrs. P., we're already in trouble, so what's a little more between friends?"

This would entail a lot of explaining to Cordelia.

When they came to the old creek bed, Quasi took her hand and pulled her up.

"You'd have to know exactly where you needed to look," Quasi said. "On a direct line, this is the approximate area for an exit, but who's to say whether there was a tunnel leading all the way to the water?"

Gracie suddenly saw that Charlie's contraption had appeared in Cordelia's driveway. "Quasi, you better get a move on!" He was too far away to spot them, she thought, but she couldn't be certain.

"I wanted to talk to him, so I'm going over there now. You hustle yourself out of here."

The boy took off in a flash. She had just pushed her way through the last of the underbrush when Charlie appeared before her.

"You lose something?" he wanted to know.

"Oh, hi, Charlie. It's all this tunnel stuff we've been learning about from Cordelia. I came to see you, but when you weren't home, somehow my curiosity drew me over here to see what she'd been talking about. I know I should have asked first."

He nodded, his expression revealing nothing. Then he looked past her in the direction from which she'd come.

"You probably heard about the thefts. . . ."

His eyes slowly swung back to her, his stare so intense it seemed to bore into her, forcing her to take a step back. She wasn't afraid of him so much, as she was embarrassed. His gaze demanded an honesty she hadn't felt prepared to give.

"Maybe you remember where the exit to the tunnel is located."

"I reckon I do," he replied.

"Charlie," she felt the urge to confess suddenly. "I am so ashamed. I was snooping in the tunnel, and discovered the blocked entrance to another house. I thought it might have something to do with the thefts."

"It's all right to be curious, Missus Parks. And you said you was sorry. I forgive you for your snooping."

"Then you'll show me the opening?"

He shook his head. "Ain't your business and it ain't safe.

Mr. Harmon used to warn us about playing there. No, it ain't smart, neither, so I'm not going to show you."

He ambled back toward the house, and she didn't know whether to stay or follow him, until he stopped in front of the pile of rocks. Charlie turned to face her. "I see you weren't the only one snooping. Those kids found Meemaw's old house, didn't they?"

She nodded, breathing a sigh of relief to have it all out in the open. Gracie followed him into the house. She found herself babbling on about Chuckie and his crew. How, looks aside, they were great kids, really.

"I am really sorry, Charlie. I shouldn't have been poking around in your past. I'm sure it's a painful memory—the fire, losing your parents."

"They're living in heaven, so, I reckon, they're happy enough. Me, I'm getting old." He looked upward. "Plumb tired. Some mornings, I say, 'Lord, take me home. I'm ready to cross the Jordan. Swing low, sweet chariot.'"

She smiled. "I like that song, too."

"'The Drinking Gourd,' do you like that one?"

"The choir is doing it for the Founders' Day worship service in the park. You've heard us practice it—you'll have to come."

"That's right. Mizz Comfort invited me to come with her family. She's going to pack a picnic lunch with fried chicken. I don't usually like going places with lots of people, but she promised she'd sew my story in a quilt, just like Meemaw's ma done for her.

He grinned broadly. "I told Mizz Cordelia that I just might go. She was surprised but glad, it seemed to me."

"Did I hear you right? Your great-grandmother made your grandmother a quilt?"

His grin faded.

Gracie sensed that avenue of discussion was being closed, so changed the topic. "Cordelia was sharing with us a little bit about her childhood. You two have known one another a long time."

"Meemaw told us that we need to look out for each other. She and Mr. Harmon were like kin. And his daddy before him."

Charlie's actions were slow and deliberate. He wiped his brow with an old handkerchief. "Yes'm, sometimes Mizz Cordelia frets over me too much, but I pay her no mind. I know it makes her feel better. She worries folks will take advantage of me."

His eyes brightened. "I tell her, that's all right, they can't take anything I wouldn't have given them anyway. Folks get confused about what they need and what they want. Sometimes I think they don't know the difference at all."

"They probably don't."

He nodded. "Worm in the radish don't think there is anything sweeter. Guess it's the same with people. No, I don't pay them no mind. There's plenty of good folks in Willow Bend. Folks who judge a man by who he is, not who he seems to be. They know something sweeter."

"Tell me about Mr. Harmon and Mr. Jasper."

"Not much to tell. They was brothers."

She smiled. "You're one of those *good* folk, Charlie Harris."

"Takes one to know one."

His smile now was pleased. "Mr. Jasper broke his back trying to save my ma and pa," his voice was barely audible. "Front porch gave way when he was going in after them."

She didn't know how to respond.

"They was good folk, too, the Marshalls."

Gracie sat quietly, not sure where the story was going, and afraid of asking him anything that would cause him to withdraw again. "Did you know their father?" she finally brought herself to say.

"He died 'fore they was born."

That threw her for a loop. "Before they were born?"

"They was twins."

"And their mother?"

He shrugged, and she sensed she'd stumbled on another forbidden topic. Gracie was now fairly certain she had found the missing piece. Now, if she could only find the place where it fit.

Gracie panicked when she spotted Jim Thompson's cruiser

by The Sweet Shoppe. Gracie feared the worst: had Charlie told Cordelia? Perhaps she'd called the police! This time, she would shoulder the blame. She didn't want to see Chuckie lose his chance at those scholarships.

Lord, keep them out of mischief, and if it's too late, make them squirm. Confession is not only good for the soul, but will go a long way with Jim Thompson.

"Gracie!" Jim smiled. "I heard our friend Chuckie is performing a little community service. Mrs. Fountain is pleased with their work. I was just telling him that if he needed a recommendation for college, I'd be happy to oblige."

She gave a sigh of relief.

"Gee, Mrs. Parks," Quasi exclaimed. "I bet you thought we were in trouble again."

She had to laugh. Was she so transparent?

"It's okay," Chuckie told her. "You're just acting like my mom, and that's not so bad."

Amy flashed Chuckie a coquettish smile. "Can we get ice cream now, Charles?"

"Charles, is it?" Jim feigned being impressed. "She's a pretty girl, Mr. Moon. You treat her right now, or you'll have her dad to contend with, as well!"

"My dad already gave him 'The Talk,' as he calls it. So don't worry, Mr. Thompson." She slipped her arm through his. "Besides, we're not going together. We're just friends."

She looked up at Chuckie. "For now, that is."

"Officer Thompson, since you're so impressed with the new us," Quasi grinned, "maybe you'll spring for the ice cream?"

"Always working the angles aren't you, Weaver?" Jim laughed.

Although her day thus far had been unsettled and unsettling, this unlikely camaraderie gave Gracie cause once again to praise God.

HERB DEFINITELY SUSPECTS ME," Comfort told Gracie.

"He came over here last night asking some more questions," Rick confirmed. "Comfort called Marybeth right after Herb left, but the woman would barely speak to her."

Gracie accepted a glass of water from Rick. "I thought things were fine between the two of you. What happened?"

"Marybeth talked to Stacy Piper, the quilt expert." Comfort took a deep breath. "It seems Stacy led Marybeth to believe that I promised the heirloom for exhibit in her show on African American quilts. But, Gracie, I didn't promise anything of the kind! If anything, I was outright evasive!

"I'd told Stacy that the woman who owned it assumed it to be her legacy, and that I wasn't ready to contradict her. She was so accommodating, how could I have known she'd show up on Marybeth's doorstep, demanding to see the quilt? I should have called and told her the quilt had been stolen."

Rick broke in now. "The woman practically accused Marybeth of robbing African Americans of their past."

"Gracie, I told you how sneaky she was," Comfort reminded her. "She got the name of our church from one of my snapshots."

"And, of course, you explained all this to Marybeth."

Comfort nodded. "I tried to, but all I got was '*mmm-hmm*,' '*umm*' and '*ah*.' That's it."

Comfort felt that Herb's politeness had hidden his real agenda. "His visit just made me so uncomfortable."

"But I don't understand...."

"He didn't out-and-out accuse me, but I kept feeling he was here because Marybeth couldn't make herself fully trust me. Still!"

Gracie shook her head.

"I just think Marybeth put him up to it," Comfort insisted. She looked at Gracie. "Now she won't really talk to me again. What I just told you I pieced together from my conversation with Stacy. Then I called Marybeth back after that, and she pretty much confirmed what the woman had told me, with her *mmm-hmms* and *ahs*. I apologized again, but to no avail. She told me she just needed time."

Comfort sighed. "Gracie, I don't know what else to do."

"Wait her out," her husband advised. "Give her time to recognize your loyalty to her in all this. It'll be okay, you'll see."

Comfort looked unconvinced. "I just want these cases solved! I still can't believe that I'm a suspect!"

"You're not, honey." Rick rubbed her back. "Herb is taking swipes at you just to humor his wife. I might do the same. The difference is I'm not the police chief."

Gracie tended to agree with Rick's assessment of the situation. "Herb is frustrated," she told them. "I could see it in his face. He's simply tired, and baffled by this whole case."

"How are you making out with your research?" Comfort asked.

"I've got a pile of pieces, but no clear idea how they fit together yet."

Lillian came into the kitchen looking for a snack, and Rick got up to quarter an apple. He fixed it with peanut butter.

"That's one of my favorite snacks, too," Gracie told the child.

"I know you didn't stop by just to hear my troubles," Comfort said, making room for Lillian in her chair. "Is there something special you needed?" She smiled. "Perhaps help with your quilt square?"

"I've thought one out, does that count?" Gracie lightened the mood. "Do you imagine I can think it onto a piece of muslin?"

Comfort chuckled. "How about you think out loud and I'll design. Sound like a plan?"

"It's probably the only way my square is going to get done."

They all laughed.

"I do have a hunch on who the thief may be, but right now it is still a long shot," Gracie said changing the subject back again.

"Well, don't keep us in suspense!" Rick said, leaning against the counter.

"Not just yet. I need to do a little more research, and I was hoping Comfort would help me with that."

"How about tomorrow?" She asked. "I have some free time."

Gracie agreed, and left the Hardings wiping peanut butter off their little girl's chin.

The next day was Saturday. Gracie knew Charlie worked in Cordelia's garden on the weekends because she'd seen him busy there often enough. She picked Comfort up at ten and they headed over to the tourist home.

"Gracie, there was a quilt. Charlie can describe it and he knows about the code. We talked about the code in the music, and I mentioned quilts. But he just clammed up when he thought I was asking too many questions."

She looked at Gracie. "Do you think Charlie knows who took the missing things?"

Gracie admitted she wasn't sure, but she thought he might.

"You don't think we should talk to Cordelia first? She practically cross-examined me after my last meeting with him."

Gracie glanced her way. "She is overprotective of him, and lately I have been wondering why. He seems to do fine on his own."

"I have to admit, Gracie, this whole thing has been absolutely fascinating. I wrote my sister a long e-mail about Willow Bend, its participation in the Underground Railroad, the discovery of the quilt, and Charlie."

She glanced at Gracie. "He does seem to hold the key. My sister, Hope, is a children's writer. I even suggested the idea of her writing his story."

"She knows how Rick and I have come to cherish our life in Willow Bend."

"Even in spite of your experience with the Bowers?"

The younger woman smiled. *"Because* of my experience. Herb put his concerns on the table, and even though Marybeth was upset, she did listen. After I thought about it, I decided that was probably the best she could do, after her experience with Stacy Piper.

"I appreciated Herb's honesty. It was hard for him to ask those questions. Remember he has to go to church with us every week."

Gracie nodded. The woman had a point there. "Problems are easier to solve when they're out in the open."

"Exactly. I was upset when you were at my house last night. Now that I've had time to think about it, I've come to value my church family even more, because of our willingness to try and work things out."

Gracie certainly agreed. She'd had the same thoughts herself.

Gracie glanced in her friend's direction, and caught Comfort studying her with a bemused expression. "What is it?"

"I'm happy to be with you. I wish my mom and I could have been close like this. Gracie, how did you get to be so wise?"

"By surrounding myself with wiser friends—present company included!" Gracie eased the Cadillac into one of the parking spaces. "Okay, Mizz Comfort, turn on the charm."

As expected, Charlie was there in the garden, aerating the soil with his spade. "I put a nice edge on this for Mizz Cordelia," he said as they approached. "Thought I'd try it out first. She don't like a heavy spade. Besides, this old thing belonged to her mama."

"Well, then, that makes it special," Comfort told him.

Charlie leaned on the spade. "What brings you ladies calling?"

"I was hoping we would have time to talk," Comfort told

him. "Remember, I asked about talking again? You've got a lot to tell us, Charlie. About our town and your family."

Charlie's eyes changed. Gracie was afraid he would again turn reluctant.

"I loved your stories about your grandmother," she said, hoping that a mention of his favorite topic might put things on a better track.

It worked. A gratified smile deepened the lines around his mouth and made his eyes seem to spark. "I can do that. Mizz Cordelia wouldn't mind at all. Why don't we sit a spell?"

Charlie led them to the rose-covered gazebo. "In summer, this place blooms with yellow roses." He smiled. "I like yellow. It's the right kind of bright."

"You're right," Comfort said. "I have to admit, though, I'm not much of a gardener—that's my husband's department. He even likes to put up the harvest—canning and freezing."

"I help Mizz Cordelia sometimes. She makes me raspberry jam. I love the smell in the kitchen when she's doing that. I used to help her mama, and Meemaw, too." He smiled. "You want to talk about her, right? That's easy for me—I loved Meemaw."

Comfort pulled out her notebook. "Did she remember being a slave? Did she tell you anything about that time?"

"My grandmother was born in 1853 on a plantation not far from Decatur, Georgia. She was 103 years old when she died.

She had a brother and daughter, they was her only kin that she knew about. Her brother lived in California. I never did know him. Her daughter was my mama."

Charlie frowned in concentration. "People sometimes act as if I don't know these things, but I do. I was born February 7, 1916, during a blizzard. Meemaw and Mizz Cordelia's mother brought me into the world. Meemaw said I was in too big a hurry to get started living, because I was a tiny thing to behold.

"My daddy went to war that year, so he wasn't there when I was born. He lost his right leg in the fighting, but Meemaw said it was his spirit that was mortally wounded. A body can live without a limb, but it shrivels up without a spirit. He liked horses more than people. Folks came from all around because he was the best blacksmith in the county."

He looked at what Comfort was writing. "Is that good?"

"*Mmm-hmm.*" She glanced up. "Let's back up a little. So, your grandmother was born before the Civil War."

"She escaped with her mama and older brother. They was all alone in the mountains. Her brother Lester killed a bear— he was only twelve years old."

He began to rock, his expression faraway. "'Wade in the water,'" be began softly. "'Wade in the water, children. Wade in the water. God's gonna trouble the water.'" Then, looking at Gracie. "I like that song, too. Think you can sing that one?"

She nodded.

He smiled at Comfort. "Your husband has a fine voice. I like to hear a black man singing 'Follow the Drinking Gourd.' Purely powerful. I wanted to do something nice for you all. Mizz Cordelia thought you'd like new choir robes."

"You're the anonymous donor?"

He put his finger to his mouth. "The left hand mustn't know what the right hand does."

"Tell me why God troubled the water," Comfort said, gently drawing him back to the subject she was most interested in. "I think that means something to you."

"Dogs. They couldn't track the runaways in the water. Meemaw walked in the water most of the way. Her mama took sick with pneumonia—almost killed her. Lester carried her to Mr. Elijah's log cabin. That was the safe house by the creek. Caretaker by the name of Lory Kindness lived there— a freeman. He married Meemaw years later."

"That was the house that burned down?" Gracie asked.

He nodded.

She touched his arm. "God spared you. And He's given you Comfort to tell their story. There is always a blessing if you wait for one. But you've had so many blessings, Charlie."

He pushed himself to stand. "You're right, Missus Parks. Now I guess the time has come to show you what's left. There's more folks over in that place than in the graveyard. You'll see, just follow me."

CHARLIE LED THEM across the property to a well-hidden opening. They entered through what seemed to be a root cellar, but Charlie explained it was a hiding place for runaways. "Black folks was less conspicuous with black folks, so Lory kept them when he could. Mr. Elijah, Lory and later Nellie would pass them between the houses when the slave hunters was near."

"I read that Elijah spent some time in jail for harboring runaways," Comfort told him.

Charlie paused at the charred plank door. "Don't know about that. Meemaw said it about killed him when his son betrayed him. Maybe that was the time."

"How did his son betray him?" Gracie asked, recalling what Rocky had deduced from the old newspaper reports. Could that son have sold his family out to the slave hunters?

The old man shrugged. "Them's skeletons you just don't rattle, Missus Parks. Meemaw never talked of the trouble he brought on the family. She just said his mother died of a broken heart, and his father swore never to remember that son."

He opened the door, and let them enter first. They stepped into a time capsule.

Charred beams attested to fire, but the room was welcoming. Charlie had created his own private museum. There were photographs of his parents, his grandmother and the Marshalls. Marybeth's quilt was draped over a rocking chair, while the Jacksons' pitcher and bowl stood on a nearby oak washstand. A straw-mat-covered wooden bed frame was in one corner. Charlie stood at the threshold, awaiting their reaction.

Gracie entered the room, delighted by its simple but charming effect. "Did all these things belong to your grandmother?"

"Yes'm." And to Comfort: "This is all that was left. I found most of the furniture when I worked for Mr. Jasper. He had me clean out the carriage house one time, and I discovered the belongings of the cabin. He said they was too painful of a reminder to Meemaw, so he kept them just in case she wanted them some day."

He paused. "I was a boy back when that fire hit us. Mr. Harmon said it wouldn't be right to rebuild here, and they was all getting on in years. Mr. Harmon never married 'til he was nearly too old. We went to live with him and Mizz Susanne in the big house so we could take care of each other."

Comfort walked around the room, running her hand over the oak table, wash stand and bureau. "Charlie, I don't know what to say. This is amazing."

"It's my place," Charlie told them. "I get lonesome for Meemaw."

Gracie's chest tightened, and her heart was full. Sometimes she sat in El's chair in his study, and could almost smell his cologne. It was consoling to sit and remember. Then, El didn't seem so far away.

"Mizz Cordelia and me use to play in here," Charlie was saying. "Weren't no furniture back then. We called this our safe place. If we was feeling blue or angry we came here. Last time Mizz Cordelia was here was the day her husband died. He didn't come home from Korea."

Charlie watched them inspect the room.

Gracie stopped at a wooden book case.

"I built it. They was Meemaw's books. Mizz Cordelia didn't even miss them." He pulled the quilt off the back, and sat down in the rocking chair. "I didn't mean no harm, only to take back what was rightfully mine."

Gracie paused beside the pitcher and bowl. "This was also your grandmother's?"

"Meemaw missed her wash bowl. Didn't know what happened to it. 'Wash up, Charlie. Don't forget behind your ears, you hear?'" He smiled, as though recalling his childhood. "Never forgot that, no, ma'am. I knew that was Meemaw's when I saw it at church."

Gracie was curious. "How did you get away with it? Did you sneak back in after the reception?"

"No, ma'am! I just carried it out. You was all talking and eating, and I just picked it up, proud as you please and walked out. Nobody took notice of me. They never do."

"And the quilt?" Comfort asked. "I suppose you did the same—just took it off with you?"

He nodded. "Didn't think I was doing wrong."

Comfort crouched beside the man. "Do you know the story of the quilt, like you know 'Wade in the Water' and 'Follow the Drinking Gourd'?"

"It's a story blanket. Meemaw's ma made it for her. She taught me the story. She made me promise to always remember. I can tell the story of the patches better than I can cipher."

He grinned. "And I'm pretty good at that. Nobody pulls one over on old Charlie Harris, no siree. But if they think they do, you know it don't matter to me. My life ain't theirs and I wouldn't want it to be."

"You and I understand pain-stitched hope, don't we, Charlie?" Comfort looked at him with affection. "This quilt is our legacy, it helped lead our people to freedom—"

"Mr. Lincoln led us to freedom. Are you testing me? I have

a book about Mr. Lincoln over there on the book shelf. Mizz Cordelia gave me a copy of the prayer book he carried in his pocket. A fine man, Mr. Lincoln."

Comfort smiled. "I'm not testing you, Charlie. You're right, Mr. Lincoln led our country to freedom. But equality has been a long time coming."

"Don't know about that. I know how to read, cipher, measure, and study the Bible, and with them, I get by fine."

Gracie smiled. "Indeed you do."

"I done a fine job with that dead wood in the churchyard, didn't I, Missus Parks?"

She nodded.

Comfort now began to quiz him on the meaning of patterns.

"'Don't you fall asleep, child!'" He laughed and hugged the quilt. "Nellie was in love with Bad Peter from almost the first day she laid eyes on him. Bad Peter was the slave that wouldn't be. Oh, no, he run away every chance he get, 'cepting they kept catching him. He'd run again soon as the wounds they'd gave him would heal. Nellie use to tend them wounds, and he told her the story of the mountains and rivers leading to freedom—to Canada."

Charlie unfolded the quilt and pointed to the centerfold. "'Follow the Drinking Gourd to mountains, sweet Nellie. Bad Peter almost made it to the river.'" Charlie pointed to the blue embroidery. "'But dogs, they sniffed him out. Wade in the water, sweet Nellie. Keep your eye on Jesus, but follow the Drunkard Path.'

"You're going to sew Meemaw's story?" Charlie asked.

Comfort nodded, her smile urging him on.

Charlie continued in his musical way, telling of Peter's successful escapes, each time taking himself a little closer to freedom. Each time, Nellie stitched a little more of his story in the quilt. But there would be no fourth time for Peter, because their master sold him. It was just months after Meemaw was born. She couldn't remember her father, but knew his story by heart. He was sold to sugar planters in the Caribbean. That was the death sentence meted out to ornery young men, who persisted in seeking freedom.

"Nellie waited till God said the time was right to run. One black night, by the light of Polaris—the North Star—she slipped away, following her Jesus to freedom. 'Cept she missed the first rendezvous, and had to go on her own. She thought she could catch the others by following Peter's map, so she and the children walked to Indiana with no one but the Lord to lead them."

There were tears in Comfort's eyes. "Charlie, your story has to be told. You will have to give this quilt back."

"You're making me a story blanket, ain't that so, Mizz Comfort?"

"That's so, Charlie. But this quilt belongs to all of us. You must give it back to Marybeth Bower. She'll do what is right, I'm sure of it."

He shook his head. "Meemaw was sad that this was lost."

"Baby, it's not lost." Comfort was crying now. "It's found! And it's nothing without your voice. You're the storyteller! It's your turn now! You have to give the quilt back."

She leaned forward to look him in the eyes. "Remember me telling you about the village storyteller, the one chosen to pass on our history? Charlie, that's you!"

Charlie reached out gently to swipe at her tears. "Don't cry, Mizz Comfort. You can have the quilt."

He handed her the heirloom. "'Follow the North Star. Freedom is across the Jordan.'"

"Amen," she whispered. "Someday you'll cross the Jordan, Charlie, and be with your parents and Meemaw. But, today, you have to tell this story."

He nodded, still rocking in the chair.

They walked Charlie home to meet Cordelia sitting in the gazebo in the back yard where they'd started. "I had a feeling you would figure it out, Gracie Parks."

"You knew, Mizz Cordelia?" Charlie took off his hat. "I didn't mean no harm. I love you like kin, but I had to do what I had to do."

She walked to meet him. "Charlie, how much did you tell

them?" Then she said to Gracie, "I'll fix us some of my minty tea. Looks like we need to talk."

Over tea, Cordelia confessed that she had suspected Charlie of taking the heirlooms. She didn't know about the furnished room in the old foundation, but she remembered their playing there as children. She'd searched his room and workshop in the basement, recalling his pack-rat habit of hiding anything he thought belonged to his family. Cordelia even knew about the missing books!

"What I don't understand," Gracie thought out loud, "is how the quilt ended up in Marybeth's family. I can understand the pitcher and bowl, but what about the quilt?"

Cordelia stirred her tea for a long moment. "Have a sugar wafer, Charlie, they're your favorite. We don't entertain nearly enough, do we?"

"No, ma'am. Your mama loved to entertain, I remember that."

She passed the plate to Gracie. "Cookie?"

"Cordelia, I would give anything to have met your parents and grandparents," Gracie said. "What they did was extraordinary. Someday when we're all in heaven together, I am going to thank them personally."

Cordelia smiled. "There is a part of our story of which I am not proud, so hold your accolades until you hear the rest.

"Velina Ames married my great-grandfather's son

Harmon. Every family has a black sheep, and ours was Harmon Marshall. He was a rogue, an unrepentant gambler, and a ladies' man. But Velina loved him, and Nellie loved her for it. Nellie practically raised Elijah's only son. She was his nanny.

"Harmon had gambling debts, so he sold out our family. He led trappers to our tunnel. There was shooting, and no one knows who did what, but it caused the tunnel to cave in on them, killing the three runaways, my grandfather and the slave trader."

She took a sip of tea, seeming to weigh her words. "Harmon and Velina were secretly married. Elijah had wanted his son to marry a girl from a good Pittsburgh family. And the Taylors, Velina's parents, did not like Quakers. At that time in history, they were considered cowards and troublemakers. Quakers refused to serve in war, and were adamant abolitionists.

"Velina's parents had *also* promised their child to someone else. When Harmon was killed, Velina had to admit she was pregnant.

"Her father paid Jared Ames to marry her. He staked their trip to California. What Marybeth doesn't know is that there were three children—a pair of twin boys to Harmon, and Jared's daughter Marissa. It was Marissa who came home with the quilt."

Cordelia paused. "Boys were desirable at that time in history, and they stayed on with a family in California. Nellie's son brought Marissa home.

"Nellie had given the quilt to Velina, hoping to protect it, because their cover had been blown by Harmon. She had no idea whether or not she would even remain a free woman, because by that time, Elijah had been charged with harboring fugitive slaves.

"Marybeth's story is correct in that Nellie's boy returned with Marissa wrapped in the quilt. He meant to give the quilt to his mother, but things got confused."

"Why didn't she ask for the quilt back?"

"She was a Negro, and afraid. The Marshall family had suffered all kinds of harassment from some of the townsfolk, and they were really worried about vigilante justice."

Cordelia smiled at Charlie. "And Nellie was a gentle woman of faith. She put the fate of that quilt in the hands of God. She often told my mother that. She was confident that it would one day return to her family. Seems it took a century and a half to come home, but it has."

Gracie glanced between Charlie and Comfort. God's ways were certainly mysterious, but his timing was always impeccable.

"The twins, young Harmon and Jasper, returned to Willow Bend as young men. Elijah embraced them as sons. No one knew the whole story, and he was too old to argue with, and too respected to contradict. The rest I think you already know. . . ."

Gracie turned the heirlooms over to Herb at the police station. "Don't ask any questions, and I'll tell you no lies."

"I've got to make a report, Gracie!"

She nodded. "An anonymous donor."

"Gracie!" Herb furrowed his brow.

"The donor was the rightful owner."

Herb shook his head. "How am I going to write that up in the police report?"

"They are anniversary gifts to the town of Willow Bend. The owner hopes they'll be put on display for everyone to enjoy."

"I don't know what Marybeth is going to say about that."

Gracie smiled. "I'm on my way to talk to her now. Would you like me to take the quilt?"

He rolled his eyes. "I suppose you plan to return the pitcher and bowl yourself to its rightful owner, as well?"

"I return them to the trustees. The rightful owner trusts them to make the right decision."

Herb threw his hands up. "I don't what I'm going to write up! I'll be darned if you don't have me totally confused!"

"Just stamp the case closed."

"Gracie, I don't know what I am going to do with you!" He shook his head. "Frankly, I don't care where you got these, I'm just glad they're back! Marybeth will be ecstatic. That's all I know!"

Gracie looked at him. He obviously wasn't finished.

"Gracie, I know you understand how hard this case was on our marriage."

She did understand how difficult it had been for Herb and Marybeth, but still that didn't excuse their behavior toward Comfort. "Comfort is the one who deserves the apology."

He lowered his head. "I was out of line."

"Yes, you were." She touched his arm. "But she's forgiving. She gets it from her Father."

He smiled. "That makes it easier."

"Have you heard any more on Carl Jackson?"

"Not much. He's small potatoes. They want the ringleaders. Ann's going to see what kind of deal she can cut for him. She's with him in Chicago now."

"Did Deborah go, too?"

He shook his head. "I think it was just Ann and Carl."

Gracie now felt her sleuth instincts could be put to rest— for the time being, at least.

THE FOUNDERS' DAY PICNIC was in full swing. It was a picture-perfect day under an azure sky, with a breeze wafting the scent of flowering trees and bushes over Fairweather Park. Uncle Miltie was right, Willow Bend had to be the closest thing to paradise this side of heaven.

Across the park was a gigantic red-and-white open tent. It would host the evening's worship and revival meeting, but now it was serving as both an arts-and-crafts fair and historical display. Charlie Harris had his own story corner, decked with the once-missing quilt. Beside it hung a parchment history, penned in calligraphy by its co-contributor, Marybeth Bower.

The heirloom coded quilt itself had been donated to the town as the centerpiece of a soon-to-be constructed log museum commemorating Willow Bend's part in the activities of the Underground Railroad. Marybeth had been so moved by its full history that she'd donated it in Nellie's honor, insisting Charlie was the quilt's rightful owner, but Cordelia had proposed the plaque list both people.

"Hey!" It was Lillian, barreling her way toward Gracie, waving a blue ribbon. "Me and daddy won!"

Rick was on her heels. "They didn't call me 'Stilts' Harding in high school for nothing! I just strapped this little cub to my leg and off we went! The rest is Willow Bend history!"

Comfort kissed him. "Just don't put your back out, Sport." Then she scooped up Lillian. "I put my money on you, sweetie. You did a great job."

"I hung on to Daddy's leg."

Comfort laughed. "Good strategy. Daddy will always be there for you, and so will I."

Gracie smiled, enjoying their love for one another and their ability to show it. "I'm so glad everything turned out all right."

"You knew it would," Comfort said. She eyed Gracie. "Now, the question remains: Did you get your square for the church quilt finished?"

Gracie hung her head.

"I'm going to get Marybeth and the two of us are coming over to your house tomorrow night!" Comfort shook her head. "You're not going to be the only one in the Eternal Hope brood without a banner or a contribution to the church quilt!"

Rick had them signed up next for the blueberry-pie-eating contest; off they went. Gracie was content to people-watch, her blanket strategically located at the best vantage point for viewing all the afternoon activities.

"Bet you're pretty pleased with yourself," Rocky said, joining her later in the day.

She smiled. "It did work out well, didn't it?"

The peanut relay was just getting organized, and they turned their attention to the commotion. Gracie studied her old friend. "You did a fine job with your story on Charlie," she complimented him.

"Like you said, he's a character, and characters make good stories." He leaned back on his elbows. "Besides that, he donated the money for a local historical exhibit, and that in itself is newsworthy. I thought it was about time Willow Bend's most bashful philanthropist was honored. But I had to promise not to divulge any other of his generous gestures."

He looked at her. "You're the one who deserves praise! How did you get the Jacksons to not only drop the lawsuit, but also donate the pitcher and bowl? Carl has certainly embraced this museum project with zeal."

"It was Deborah's doing, really," Gracie told him. "But Ann McNeil's stepping in as Carl's attorney didn't hurt."

"Pretty amazing," Rocky said, "that our new museum owes its existence to Charlie Harris, who gave the money needed to excavate and renovate the foundation. It's some sort of full circle, that's for sure."

He chuckled. "You're something, Gracie Parks. You really are. I always find new reasons to think so."

"I need a partner for the peanut race." It was Marge standing above them. "Gracie, no offense, but I don't want to go nose to nose with you. Come on, Rocky, it'll be good for your humility."

Abe Wasserman was behind her. "What do you say, Gracie? Should we try to take the blue ribbon in this event?"

The tent was packed, the choirs sitting front and center. Personally, Gracie thought Eternal Hope's choir the most handsome, their new ivory robes accented by gold metallic stoles. Estelle sat majestically robed in Don's garb, and their modest chemistry teacher smiled, his tea-length gown happily hidden by two rows of his peers.

Rick Harding took his position as soloist in a medley of spirituals, featuring both "Follow the Drinking Gourd" and "Wade in the Water." Gracie's spirits soared, and the massed choir clapped and swayed to the music while the congregation joined in.

Charlie Harris had been right: The harmony of the chorus combined with Rick's compelling tenor offered to everyone listening an experience that was "purely power."

When they sat down for the sermon, Gracie noticed Amy had her eye on a handsome young man in a tie. Chuckie! The boy evidently noticed her watching because he lowered his head. Gracie suspected he was covering his blush.

The Bowers were sitting next to the Hardings, and Casey held Lillian on her lap. Charlie Harris was next to Comfort, Cordelia on the other side of him. Phyllis Nickolson was rocking her baby, and Terry had his arm around Katie. Gracie bowed her head and thanked God for beautiful weather and a family for all seasons.

When she opened her eyes, she spied a burly man in a dress shirt without a tie fidgeting in the seat next to Abe Wasserman. Rocky caught her gaze and flashed a shy grin.

Her cup ran over, Gracie decided. And if Willow Bend was so close to heaven, as Uncle Miltie kept saying, then there wasn't really any reason why Rocky couldn't be one of the angels.

Gracie's Tasty Lasagna

- ✓ 1/2 pound lasagna noodles
- ✓ Olive oil
- ✓ Two 14 1/2 ounce cans chopped tomatoes
- ✓ Salt and pepper
- ✓ 2 cups small-curd cottage cheese
- ✓ Approxmately 2/3 pound mozzarella

- ✓ 1 1/2 cups grated Parmesan
- ✓ 2 eggs
- ✓ Approximately 2/3 cup buttered breadcrumbs
- ✓ 2 to 3 medium zucchini
- ✓ 2 medium red onions

Says Gracie, "Rocky, of course, prefers it when I add a combination of ground meat and sausage to the filling layers. But if it's just Uncle Miltie and me around the kitchen table, I opt instead for the vegetarian variation.

"Mix eggs and cottage cheese together well in a bowl. Set aside. Slice mozzarella thinly, and set that aside on a plate, too. Pour the two cans of tomatoes into a bowl (just to make things easier). Chop unpeeled zucchini and red onions into small cubes. Then, using two tablespoons of olive oil in a heavy pan, sauté them lightly together until they're just soft.

"Boil the noodles in salted water with two tablespoons of olive oil. When the noodles are soft (but not mushy), drain them.

"Lightly oil a twelve-inch baking dish and begin by laying down the first single layer of noodles, overlapping each one slightly. On top of this put some of the egg and cheese mixture, then the vegetables, with spoonfuls of the tomatoes to fill in any spaces, and finally the slices of mozzarella. Very lightly salt and pepper, then top with grated Parmesan before going on to the next layer. The top layer should be the vegetables and tomatoes topped with the mozzarella slices and grated Parmesan. I also like sprinkling buttered breadcrumbs across the top.

"Bake in a 350-degree oven for thirty to thirty-five minutes. Then stick it under the broiler to brown for a minute or so.

"Let it sit five to ten minutes before cutting portions. It serves four generously, with leftovers that taste even better."

About the Author

"I, like Gracie, love homemaking and cooking," writes ROBERTA UPDEGRAFF. "I married my high-school sweetheart, have been married for more than twenty-five years and have three-plus wonderful children. I say plus because our home seems to sprout teenagers and young adults, making our dinner table banter quite lively. This year we will host our second exchange student, and we've just returned from a lovely reunion with his predecessor, our new Italian son.

"I am a substitute teacher at Williamsport High School in Pennsylvania, and I love my students! I have taught everything from auto mechanics to orchestra. I am also a Sunday school teacher and volunteer youth leader. Obviously, I enjoy teenagers.

"I am a genealogy buff and storyteller, so I especially treasure family history. There is actually an Underground Railroad escape tunnel in the basement of the Updegraff family homestead.

"We continue our family's tradition by serving God as volunteers in mission. This summer we will return to Honduras for the third time to help with the ongoing reconstruction after Hurricane Mitch. We especially look forward to seeing our new friends in Honduras. This time my husband is hoping to drive to Honduras in a school bus loaded with much needed supplies.

"I am a member of the St. David's Christian Writers' Conference board of directors, and I am active in West Branch Christian Writers. This is my third book in the 'Church Choir Mysteries' series, and I continue to write for publications like *Moody*, *Focus on the Family* and *Group Magazine*."

A NOTE FROM THE EDITORS

This original Guideposts Book was created by the Book and Inspirational Media Division of the company that publishes *Guideposts*, a monthly magazine filled with true stories of hope and inspiration.

Guideposts is available by subscription. All you have to do is write to Guideposts, 39 Seminary Hill Road, Carmel, New York 10512. When you subscribe, each month you can count on receiving exciting new evidence of God's presence, His guidance and His limitless love for all of us.

Guideposts Books are available on the World Wide Web at www.guidepostsbooks.com. Follow our popular book of devotionals, *Daily Guideposts,* and read excerpts from some of our best-selling books. You can also send prayer requests to our Monday morning Prayer Fellowship and read stories from recent issues of our magazines, *Guideposts, Angels on Earth,* and *Guideposts for Teens.*